HIDDEN
BY
JADE

CELINE JEANJEAN

This book is a work of fiction. The characters, incidents and dialogue are drawn from the author's imagination and are not to be construed as real. Any resemblance to actual events or persons, living or dead, is coincidental.

ISBN: 9782492523281

Hidden by Jade
http://celinejeanjean.com

Cover by: bonobobookcovers.com
Editing by: copybykath.com

JOIN MY NEWSLETTER

AND RECEIVE THESE FREE STORIES

Subscribe to Celine Jeanjean's newsletter and receive these three novellas for free!

Go to:

http://celinejeanjean.com/freebook

1

D on't get me wrong, I love my house. I really do. I put a lot of work into making it look as nice as it does, and normally when I have some time off work, I really like hanging out here.

I've got a lovely little courtyard where my various rescue animals live, and with the vines that now somehow grow out of my walls to make a canopy,, thanks to Zer, there's some very pleasant shade.

Definitely no bad thing when summer is getting into full swing. Panong can get proper sweltering, especially given the humidity. You can step out your front door and go from freshly showered to sweaty mess in a couple of minutes in the height of summer. I'm not exaggerating.

Summer is not when I look my best.

So yeah, my courtyard is really lovely these days. All the more so when I have some Timi Yuro wafting out the doors. Timi and lazy summer days go well together. And it helps that my record player—a real find, from 1910, which I spent *ages* connecting to and gently nudging with my magic— honestly has the best sound I've come across.

In normal times I'd be happy as a clam, pottering in my courtyard. Later, I'd poke around my spice cabinet (it's seriously well-stocked. I'm a whizz in the kitchen, and yes, I do say so myself), breathing in all those mouth-watering, pungent smells, deciding what to cook for the night, maybe changing the music to something a bit more energetic.

Except that all this is far more enjoyable when I have *chosen* to be home alone. It's quite different when I'm under house arrest.

Okay, so I'm not *technically* under house arrest. I could walk out if I wanted to. If I was suicidal, that is.

Because the moment I set foot outside of my house, the problem of Yue rears its sickeningly polished and beautiful head. Even though she and I have made a deal, I'm not stupid enough to trust her any further than I can throw her. Now I work out, and I take pride in my strength. But firstly, I'm pretty sure that if I picked Yue up, I wouldn't survive the encounter. And even if I *did* survive, I doubt I'd be able to do more than dump her at my feet.

I know, I'm taking that metaphor too literally. That is what happens when you have spent several weeks locked away on your own with only your animals for company. You start to talk to yourself, and you find the most random thing interesting. This is a necessity because the alternative is to be bored out of your *mind.*

I don't recommend it.

The reason I'm so wary of Yue is because the deal we made involves her leaving me alive, in exchange for which I try to change Sarroch's mind about her. Sarroch, who, according to Mr Sangong, has feelings for *me.*

Yeah.

That has 'Apiya dies a slow and painful death' written all over it, which is why I'd happily trade in my situation for a

Gordian knot, but alas, no one is interested in that trade. At some point Yue will realise I can't deliver, and then my life will suddenly have considerably less value.

As if that wasn't troublesome enough, there's the rather nebulous matter of what's going on with the Mayak Elders. Neither Sarroch nor Mr Sangong will tell me anything concrete, but by all accounts, whatever is going on is not going too well.

Sarroch went to them to try to secure me some kind of status among Mayak society in order to keep me safe from future attacks from Yue, because he feels responsible for her trying to rip my throat out—seeing as she's *his wife*. Well, not his wife, but there's no human word for what she is to him, so 'wife' is the closest thing.

The problem is that since I'm not recognised as part of the Mayak, at the moment anyone can kill me any time they want without any consequences, so long as they do it discretely. Leaving Yue free to boil bunnies to her heart's content.

However, although all of this is very directly connected to me, Sarroch and Mr Sangong have been refusing to give me any updates. They seem to have mistaken me for some damsel in distress, to be locked away in her metaphorical tower while they go out into the world and sort everything out.

Not my jam. Not my jam at all, in fact.

Either that or they think I'm a mushroom—you know the old joke. They leave me in the dark and feed me shit. Haha and all that.

Christ, I really need to get out of the house. I'm plumbing new depths in the lame joke department.

My phone beeps, and I pounce on it with the enthusiasm of Hunter discovering a piece of cheese on the floor. Contact from the outside world!!

Hunter looks up at me from where he's been dozing in the shade. Having established that my phone beeping will not result in a treat for him, he goes back to sleep.

It might not be a treat for him, but it is for me. I swipe my phone to life, expecting one of the silly memes Chai has been sending me to distract me. But the message isn't from Chai.

It's from Sarroch. He's outside.

He can't come into my house anymore, not since Mr Sangong put security spells in place to keep Yue and all other Mayak out. Since Sarroch and Yue's magic is bonded, Sarroch is also unable to enter the house now. He's come to see me a couple of times since my de facto house arrest, always messaging me first to notify me that he's outside.

With him there, I'm as safe outside as I am inside the house. Even if someone attacks, he'll be able to keep them at bay. And by someone, I mean Yue. Unfortunately, Sarroch flat out refuses to take me anywhere beyond my front porch, deeming it too much of a risk.

Still, beggars can't be choosers. I fall over myself in my eagerness to reach the door. No, don't read too much into that—I'm just happy for some human interaction and a distraction from my own thoughts.

"Hi Sarroch!" I sound as perky as a cheerleader. Just give me some pompoms.

Sarroch's standing just beyond my porch, dressed surprisingly casual for him—jeans and a light grey t-shirt that does a very good job of hinting at the muscle beneath without ostentatiously showing it off. I approve.

Except of course I'm not thinking about all that.

It seems best for my survival to keep myself as far removed as possible from the whole mess that is the Sarroch situation. I'm not completely confident in Mr Sangong's evaluation that Sarroch has feelings for me, either, and I don't want to get myself humiliated again, not after Sarroch made it clear nothing will *ever* happen between us.

"Hi Api—"

Hunter barrels past me, bounding over to Sarroch, greeting him like he's a long lost best friend. Don't read anything into that, either. Hunter would greet Yue excitedly if she came regularly enough. His memory is poor and his ability to forgive is limitless, bless him.

"Down, Hunter," Sarroch orders. His voice comes out deeper and more resonant than normal.

My jaw practically hits the floor when Hunter obeys. Seriously? Years, I've had Hunter—*years*—and he's never obeyed a verbal command of mine.

"Good boy," Sarroch tells him, still in that deep voice that feels tinged with power. Hunter wags his plumed tail enthusiastically. Sarroch's expression relaxes into a smile, and he strokes Hunter's head.

He looks up at me. "Do you mind if I give him a treat?"

"Go right ahead."

Sarroch produces a clear plastic zip-lock back from his back pocket. Inside it are little brown biscuits of some sort.

Hunter, with his golden retriever's innate ability to spot an incoming treat, pushes his head forward as far as he can without lifting his ass from the floor, his gaze turning laser-focused.

Sarroch opens the bag.

"Bloody hell," I protest. "What the hell is that? It reeks worse than a day-old corpse."

"Have you been around many day-old corpses?" Sarroch asks with a raised eyebrow, pulling out a biscuit.

Hunter's plumed tail is now wagging at such a pace that it's doing a very thorough job of cleaning the ground. Sarroch gives him the biscuit, which Hunter gulps down so fast he can't have tasted anything.

Sarroch pulls out another and makes a low noise in his throat. "Wait."

Hunter actually waits, even when Sarroch presents the treat right in front of his nose.

"How the hell are you doing that?" I ask him, genuinely amazed. "I took him to an expensive dog trainer who couldn't get those results from him. Couldn't even get him to sit on command, in fact."

"He's responding to my tiger. He can tell I'm the alpha in his situation."

I snort. "Great. I'm not even the alpha of my own household."

Sarroch gives me a look that's like the human equivalent of the looks Tim gives me on a regular basis, but mixed with a teasing gleam. "Surely Tim has already explained that when there's a feline involved, a human is never the alpha."

"Oh, he has expounded on that subject many times."

Sarroch gives Hunter the second biscuit and then strokes his head some more. "That's it for now. And no more jumping on me."

They say the way to a woman's heart is through her stomach—and that's totally true in my case. But *they* don't mention the other shortcut, which is through bonding with a woman's dog. There's something quite disarming about watching Sarroch and Hunter get along.

It's especially endearing to see Sarroch stroke Hunter,

given that Sarroch's a powerful weretiger who could probably kill us all with a thought, while Hunter is...Hunter.

Anyway, I'm supposed to stay detached from all that.

"Any updates?" I ask. "Is freedom on the horizon at long *last*?"

Sarroch sits on the floor and leans against one of the pillars supporting the arches of the covered porch.

All houses in Old Town are like this. The pavement in front of the houses is covered by the upper floor protruding from the rest of the house. Arches help support the jutting part of the building. Partitions cut through with arches separate out my part of the pavement from my neighbours'.

The setup also means that in rainy season, people can walk along the pavement without getting wet.

Everyone tends to keep their scooters, bicycles, or other things stored beneath their porch, and it's where I keep my motorbike parked, too.

I sit against the other pillar, facing Sarroch.

"There's still a lot of arguing," he says. "Getting anything done with the Mayak takes time."

"What are the arguments, exactly?"

"You know I can't tell you that, Apiya."

I snort with annoyance. "It's not like I'm asking you to divulge Mayak state secrets. This relates to me directly. Surely I have a right to know what is being said about me."

"In any other circumstance you'd be right, but that logic won't apply to the Mayak. And I don't want to make things worse by telling you things I shouldn't. That might antagonise Mayak who are on the fence."

"On the fence about what? No, let me guess, you can't tell me."

"I'd risk making things worse."

"Meaning they're already bad?"

Sarroch looks away. "I, er..." He clears his throat. "I messed up a little. I'm confident I can fix it, but it's not worth taking the risk of further complicating matters."

"Mr Sangong hinted that you might have been a little... emotional." He did a lot more than hint, telling me that Sarroch was getting his emotions publicly tangled up over me, and that it was bad news. The Mayak have a very low opinion of emotional displays, referring to it as 'displaying the heart of a child'.

Sarroch grimaces and doesn't meet my eye. "Yes, I might have. I have it under control now, though. And I promise you I'll get something sorted out."

My heart beats a little faster. So Mr Sangong was right? Wait, no. Just because Sarroch has emotions relating to this thing with the Mayak Elders doesn't necessarily mean emotions about *me*, and even if he does, it doesn't mean he'll ever act on it. He was clear about that before.

More importantly than how Sarroch feels, it's clear my time in house purgatory isn't coming to an end anytime soon.

2

Sarroch and I fall into a slightly awkward silence. We don't yet know each other well enough to comfortably share silence, I guess.

I scramble for something I could say to him about Yue to help matters there. Showing Yue some progress with Sarroch might be the best way to end my purgatory.

The problem is that I have no idea what to say. I haven't told Sarroch about the deal I made with her. I worry that if I do, that will make things more complicated by making him angry—or more angry—with her.

If that happens, my chances of remaining alive will drop dramatically, because she'll realise I can't deliver on the deal.

Don't get me wrong, I'm not suddenly so confident in my powers of persuasion and manipulation that I think I can actually change Sarroch's mind about Yue. Rather, I need to find a way to manage the situation, keep it from crashing down on me while I figure out how to get myself out of the way.

Until I do, I'm keeping the deal to myself.

It feels a bit shitty, though, keeping that from Sarroch. Especially given how open he's been with me about his past and everything.

And that's not all I'm keeping from him. I also haven't told him what I've discovered about myself and Qinglong. He still doesn't know what I truly am.

Mr Sangong told me to keep it to myself for now, and I know better than to go against what he suggests. He wants to have a better handle on the consequences of making the reveal before putting the information out there.

So I'm keeping that secret from Sarroch too. Which means he doesn't know about my little trip to the Akha village, either.

"Is that Timi Yuro playing?" Sarroch asks.

The front door is still open, and Timi is belting out *Make the World Go Away*. Her voice really is incredible, so deep for a woman that it's nearly masculine.

"Got it in one," I tell Sarroch.

"If you like her, I'll bring you a record next time I come over that you should like."

"Oh well, if you like her, I have a new singer I recently discovered—hold on, I'll go and put the record on."

I hurry back into the house. It takes me just a second to locate the record—yes, my records are sorted alphabetically and by musical genre—and I slip it on.

"Do you know this one?" I call out as the music starts.

"Actually, I don't think so."

"Doesn't surprise me," I reply as I head back outside. "It's a brand-new singer, but the way he records his music and the way he sings, you'd think his music was released a good seventy or eighty years ago. He's an independent, and he only just put out an LP."

Sarroch taps his foot as he listens to the record. "It's good. I'll take the name from you."

I smile at that. Recommending music to people is one of my favourite things.

We listen to music for quite a while longer, playing a sort of game where I tried to find songs Sarroch doesn't know. His music collection is extensive, and I only manage to find one more he doesn't already have.

It's fun, actually, and it's such a welcome distraction.

He leaves as the sun starts to set, promising to come back tomorrow.

And he does, in the early afternoon, bearing records so we can continue our musical game. The heat is ramping up, so I make us some refreshing cocktails (of the delicious variety, not the stomach-curdling concoctions Chai is so fond of)—gin and tonic, mojito, that kind of thing.

"You're *sure* you can drive safely when you've had a drink?" I ask him for the third time as I hand him a second old-fashioned.

He grins and takes the glass from me. "Perk of being a weretiger. With my metabolism I'd have to drink the whole barrel of whiskey before I felt a little tipsy, and even then it wouldn't last more than a few moments."

"Okay. But still drive slowly just to be safe. I don't want to be responsible for an accident, and I've seen how you drive."

Sarroch raises an eyebrow. "I've piloted jet planes and driven racing cars. I can handle a regular car across Old Town."

Hard to retort to that. "So what's the next record?"

Some of the records Sarroch has brought are so ancient and weird there's no way I would have come across them before.

One I am surprised to find I particularly like is a Mongolian heavy metal band who uses traditional Mongolian throat singing where they make multiple notes at a time. Metal is not my kind of music normally, but it's raw and primal in a way that speaks to something inside me.

"It feels like hearing the harshness of the Gobi Desert in musical form," I tell Sarroch.

He smiles. "That's exactly why I like it so much. I don't know how, but something about it perfectly captures the desert. Have you been?"

"To the Gobi? No." It's amusing how casually Sarroch asks this, as if popping to the Gobi desert was on par with popping down to the wet market. Especially given it's supposed to have one of the harshest climates on earth. "But since I'm unlikely to go in the near future, I'd best get myself a copy of that record instead and go there vicariously."

"Keep it. It's a gift."

"Seriously? Thank you!"

"Actually, all the records I brought were supposed to be gifts, but you have more of them than I expected."

I'm touched. Genuinely touched. No one's bought me records before without me first telling them exactly what to buy. Either that or they buy me stuff I have already or that makes my ear bleed.

"That's what happens when you're a music nerd," I reply, trying to go for nonchalant, but not managing the tone quite right. "But seriously, you don't have to give me records. It's—"

"Apiya, these are gifts," Sarroch says gently. "It's very rude to refuse a gift from the Mayak."

I grin. "Well in that case, I gratefully accept."

"Glad to hear it."

I predict a lot of listening to music in my near future.

We talk for a while longer about music, and Sarroch

shares some entertaining tales of the time he spent in the Gobi desert as we listen to the Mongolian metal band again.

It's really good fun, getting to chat music with someone who's as much of a nerd as I am, and whose tastes run similar to mine. Given my distaste of anything electronic, most modern music just doesn't appeal to me, and I find the stuff in the charts about as pleasant to listen to as drinking perfume would be.

Sarroch eventually leaves, and I head back inside to find the right spot in my library for my new records. I'm pleasantly buzzed from the cocktails, giddy from the new records, and just generally...content. Which I haven't really felt since Yue's attack when she almost ripped my throat out.

I put the Mongolian band on and organise the other records.

I've just finished putting them away when there's a loud thump at the door. And then another.

I frown. That can't be Sarroch. Mr Sangong's spell means he can't get past the arches at the front of my house.

Maybe it's Chai, although he hadn't planned to come for a few hours yet and he normally messages to tell me he's on his way. Anyway, it can't be a Mayak given the security spells, so as I head to the door I'm feeling pretty confident in my safety.

That feeling of safety doesn't last very long when I find that standing beyond the porch is Yue. At the foot of my door are two stones that she must have thrown to attract my attention.

. She's stunning as always in a turquoise halter-neck fifties summer dress, a lace parasol providing dappled shade over her flawless porcelain skin. The fifties sunglasses and perfect waves in her hair make her look like a movie star.

"Sarroch's come to visit you two days in a row," she says,

removing her sunglasses and revealing dark, intense eyes. Her red lipstick is flawless, but behind it her teeth are sharper than razors. "Have you made progress?"

I really hope that the pontianak can't identify a lie. "It's slow, but then again you can't expect something like that to change instantly. I think we're headed in the right direction, though."

Yue's eyes gleam eagerly. "But you think there *has* been progress?"

I wonder if she realises how desperate she appears. Suddenly I feel seriously guilty for not having said anything to Sarroch about her, and for having simply enjoyed his company these last two days.

"It's too early to really tell. It will take time." I try to keep it as vague as possible. The last thing I need is for her to start setting deadlines.

But I feel sad for her. She's beautiful and powerful – surely she should be able to have her pick of the crop from the Mayak, and yet here she is, at my doorstep, hoping for a scrap of attention from Sarroch.

"If you think that anything has changed, let me know at once." She bends gracefully to the floor and places a black square just beyond the limits of my porch. "That's my phone number." She hesitates and then produces a phone from her purse.

My phone. The phone that she stole from me the day she came into my house to attack me.

Lucky I'm as anal about backing up my data as I am about cleaning, so I was able to secure a replacement phone and keep all of my contacts, but still. If it's a right pain when you lose your phone, it's even more of a pain when you've lost your phone because a homicidal and jealous pontianak stole it when she tried to kill you.

She holds my gaze for a few heartbeats. I keep my expression on the cold side of neutral. I'm certainly not going to thank her for returning it.

"I won't apologise," she says softly. "You know that, right?"

I cross my arms and press my lips into a line. Of course I wasn't expecting an apology, but then she can't expect a reply to that statement.

"I'm returning this as a gesture of goodwill," she says, placing the phone next to the card. She looks up at me as she stands back up in one fluid movement. "And as a reminder. You are only alive because *I* choose to let it be so. So I want progress—something I can see for myself. Otherwise I may decide that our deal doesn't have sufficient value for me."

"Threatening people isn't the best way to get them to cooperate with you."

"I think you'll find it's an extremely powerful motivator."

"Is it? Because last I checked Mr Sangong's spell prevents you from getting anywhere near me."

Yue bares her teeth. "I got to you once, I can get to you again."

I feel a spike a fear and adrenaline as my body reacts to the presence of a predator so close by. The spot she tore open at the side of my neck throbs in recognition, even if there's no scar there.

It goes without saying that the guilt and sadness I felt for her a moment ago has just evaporated.

"Getting to me and killing me are two different things," I snap. "And last I checked, you have yet to achieve killing me. And you might want to reconsider the threats, or *I* might decide that this deal with you is not of sufficient value for *me.* I could always leave you to sort your mess out with

Sarroch. You can keep the phone, I had the sim card cancelled when you took it, so it's useless, anyway."

I turn back and slam the door before she has the chance to reply. Let her stew on that.

For all my bravado, my hands are shaking, and my heart is pounding fast. Hunter whines and pokes his head out from behind the sofa.

So much for me thinking he'd be able to forgive Yue for breaking his leg.

"She's not getting back in here," I tell him, wishing I believed it. There's still so much I don't know about the Mayak and magic in general. What if Yue finds a way around Mr Sangong's defences? He's not invulnerable, after all. At least I don't think so.

I take a breath.

Next time I see Sarroch I will genuinely try to make some kind of progress about Yue. It was stupid to just enjoy myself these last couple of days. Softening him towards her in any way might end up being the thing that keeps me alive.

I close my eyes and lean my head back against the door. Sarroch's record suddenly grates on my nerves, and I march to the record player and turn it off.

3

Dealing with Yue and all those problems isn't the only thing on my plate. Why make your life simple when you can make it complicated, eh?

Today will end up being a very sociable day—lucky me —Chai's coming over later. But this time it's not a purely social call. Well, Chai thinks it is, but *I've* got an agenda.

First, though... I hate the fear that pulses through my veins as I hover by my front door, trying to work up the courage to open it again.

"Damn Yue," I mutter.

I yank the door open abruptly, jumping aside so I'm not in the doorway.

Yue's nowhere to be seen. The cold feeling in my guts makes me want to creep out and back in fast as I can so I can securely bolt my door again. As if I were some kind of mouse, scurrying to keep out of sight of the cat.

It's humiliating, so I force myself to move slowly, ignoring the sudden increase in my heart rate as I step beyond the threshold.

"Mr Sangong's spells work until the end of my porch," I

whisper below my breath. "Mr Sangong's spells work until the end of my porch."

I pick up my phone and Yue's business card. I don't want to take it with me, but if I leave it out, Chai will see it. Worse, Sarroch might come back unexpectedly, and there's no good way I can explain why his homicidal wife came by, not without telling him about our deal.

I swear I can feel eyes on my back as I go back inside, but I resist the urge to look back over my shoulder.

I sag with relief as I lock the door, and then go put the phone away in a drawer. As to the business card... I can't tear it up and throw it in the bin, since it's made of some kind of metal. I think. It's paper thin, black and hard, with Yue's name embossed in silver. Beneath is a real Panongian phone number.

I half expected something magical. Against my better judgement, I reach for it with my magic, just to see. I get a sense of the card, cool and slick. And there's a faint buzzing to it that's like a distant echo of the licking-a-battery feeling I get from places like the Crane, when there's a lot of magic in the air. But it doesn't feel like it's coming from the card itself. Rather, probably a residue from being handled by Yue.

I don't dare push any further. For now, though, the card seems harmless enough. I'll ask Mr Sangong about how to dispose of it.

I place the business card in the drawer and close it. I have a lot to do before Chai arrives, and between Sarroch and Yue, I'm in danger of running late.

I want to butter Chai up, which means making him a proper English cream tea.

I make a *mean* raisin scone.

I couldn't secure clotted cream, but I'm improvising by

whipping up some regular cream. The jam is strawberry, as it should be, and I ordered it from this super expensive deli.

Chai loves anything that reminds him of England. I'm even serving him some Yorkshire tea (Yorkshire Gold, of course), making use of the few remaining tea bags I still have from my parents' last visit. And of course the conversation will have to cover the weather along with a spirited debate over whether cream or jam goes on the scone first.

I don't think it's possible for a Brit to have a scone and not debate this crucial topic. Chai has never explained why cream teas make him so happy, but I'm a fan of anything that makes him smile as widely as when he's faced with a plate of freshly baked scones.

I've just finished laying everything neatly out on the table (I like to use traditional Panongian crockery as a nice counter to all the Englishness—plus the blue and white patterns on the porcelain are really pretty), and the kettle is boiling on the stove when he knocks. The message announcing his impending arrival beeped fifteen minutes ago.

"It's Chai," he calls through the door.

I smile as I take the kettle off the heat. The scene is set.

He's bound to say yes.

~

"No. Flat no. I'm trying to decide if you're being remarkably stupid, or if your sense of humour has grown warped." Chai dips his knife into the jam dish and spreads the jam over the clotted cream already thickly laid out on the scone.

I ended up agreeing with him that clotted cream should go first just to make him smile. Obviously, it wasn't enough.

"Chai, you know I'm being serious. I just need to know that Ilmu is okay."

He takes a bite of his scone, followed by a sip of tea. "So have someone else go check on her."

"Look, Ilmu has been banished from Mayak society." I try to sound as reasonable and logical as I can. "Which means that no one gives a crap about her. No one but me."

Chai shakes his head. "I'm not taking you there." He goes for more jam. The ratio of jam to scone is growing dangerously high. Daring, especially for a man in a white shirt.

"Come on, Chai. You like Ilmu."

"I'm not putting you in danger for her sake."

Did I mention that Chai's stubborn? The fact that I've come regrettably close to dying a few times recently doesn't help my case, either. These days Chai seems to have promoted himself from best friend to senior nursemaid— another one who mistakes me for a damsel in distress.

Hunter comes up to me with a toy and whines. He's clearly bored, and he wants some attention, but this is too important to let him distract me, so I shoo him away.

Chai attacks the other half of his scone. "Doesn't it creep you out that she ate your memories?"

"She did it at Mr Sangong's request. Well, Mr Sangong and my, er..." I still can't think of Qinglong as my mother, even though I'm technically her daughter. 'Maker' sits a bit better, but even that's still a bit too weird for comfort.

It's something I'm leaving for future me to process. I have too much going on at the moment.

"Qinglong requested it as well," I continue. "Ilmu did what she did to help keep me alive. That's why I need to know that she's okay. What she did to help me caused her to get banished by her own kind, and she's had to live with that all these years. So given her sacrifice, if I have any cause to be worried about her well-being—which I do since she's been incommunicado for a couple of weeks, now—I can't just do nothing."

"No. Just no, Api. Find some other way. Is your memory so bad you can't remember what happened the last time you ventured outside?"

"As far as I can remember, it all ended pretty well, actually. I'm still here, I'm still—"

"You could have died. Again. It's like you're trying to make a habit of putting your life in danger."

"Hey, you're being unfair. It's not my fault, is it? It's not like I go around—"

"Actually, that's exactly what you do. You do go around, Api. You could have stayed home instead of going to the Akha village. That was what I wanted to do, if you remember. Instead we went out, and Yue attacked us."

"Yes, and you were amazing at keeping her at bay. And if I'd done as you suggested and stayed home, I still wouldn't know anything about my magic, or about what I am."

"You would have found out, eventually. Mr Sangong would have told you."

"You know damn well he couldn't have because of the spell preventing him from speaking."

"Look, I don't want to argue over this with you. I'm not escorting you out, and that's final."

I'm seriously annoyed. So annoyed that if it wouldn't be embarrassingly petty, I'd remove the rest of the scones.

I meant all that I said about Ilmu. I really want to make sure she's okay. The fact that she's been missing for a few weeks now makes me feel proper worried. And I hate, I *hate* how useless and helpless I've become that I can't do anything to check in on her.

If a friend's in trouble and needs help, I do something about it. That's what I *do*. It's who I am. I am not the kind of person who sits on the sidelines, and I'm certainly not someone who likes to be coddled and cosseted.

I look away so I don't glare at Chai. It wouldn't be very fair since I know he's doing what he thinks is best for me, and he's been pretty amazing at coming to visit regularly and generally helping make sure I don't lose my mind from being stuck at home.

As I glance aside, I catch sight of Hunter. The split second it takes me to process what he's doing is too slow.

"Hunter, no!"

He's been trying to ease one of his toys from behind a potted succulent plant that's up on a small table. The plant has long limbs that cascade over the pot's edge, each one heavy with little succulent pods. The pot is a beautiful piece of glazed ceramic. The toy is a plaited thing that has turned all snaggly from Hunter's chewing.

You can see where this is going.

By the time I've stood up and said the words, Hunter has already yanked his toy, which catches on the plant's limbs.

The pot crashes to the floor sending soil, broken pottery, and bits of succulent all over the place. Hunter yelps and jumps back, looking startled.

Chai leaps to his feet, all the metal cutlery on the table shooting up in the air and turning into sharp blades.

"Dammit, Hunter," Chai mutters as the cutlery returns to its natural form and back to its place.

Hunter jumps a few more paces back and looks back and forth between me and the pot. He looks agitated.

I frown at him, and he goes and sits quietly in a corner with his head down. His version of mea culpa.

"Well, saved by the bell," Chai says, stretching his arms

above his head. "I'll let you clean that up—I need to get back to my studio."

Now, I cannot overstate just how anal I am when it comes to cleanliness. Having soil and broken ceramic all over my floor, to say nothing about the damage to my plant, could make me break out in hives if I don't deal with it quickly.

I turn away from the carnage. *That's* how serious I am about checking in on Ilmu.

"Great idea," I tell Chai. "I'll come with you, and we can swing by the University on the way."

Chai rolls his eyes. "Api, come on—"

I grip both his elbows. "Chai, enough of the joking and pussyfooting around the issue. The last time I saw Ilmu she was with other baku, because they were dealing with Akiho, the unstable baku who worked with Nerong. What if they're also doing something to *her*? What if they believe her unstable because she can't tell them who I am or why she ingested my memories? I already feel incredibly bad that she was banished as a consequence of helping keep me alive. If something else has happened to her because of me, and I do nothing, I'll never forgive myself."

"What if it's nothing to do with you?"

"That could be the case," I admit.

"Don't you see that the risk is too great?"

I shake my head. "No. She's a friend who might need help. I don't turn away from that. Risk or no risk. I just don't. I'd do the same for you, and you know it."

Chai glares at me. "Dammit, Api. You only get to pull that card once, you hear?"

"If Ilmu is in her office, we come straight home, and I never ask to leave again. Not until Mr Sangong says it's safe. I *promise*."

4

Even before I knock on Ilmu's door, something doesn't feel right. Like a shiver of warning down my spine. And when my intuition speaks, it's always right.

We're in the virtually empty part of Panong University that Ilmu has been inhabiting the whole time I've known her. The rest of the University has been renovated and modernised but this part has somehow been forgotten about. Maybe it's part of a baku's magic.

There are three doors in the part of the corridor we're standing in. The one at the end is Ilmu's door, the other two are closed. Next to each one is a nameplate holder that would normally have held some kind of card indicating the name of the office occupant. Both holders are as empty as the corridor, dust having accumulated in the runners.

There is no nameplate at Ilmu's door.

That's not what has me bothered, though. It's something else, something I can't put my finger on. A subtle wrongness. And I don't mean the wrongness of knowing I left a mess of soil and broken ceramic on my floor.

Yes, that is how much this kind of thing bothers me—I can't stop thinking about it.

But the wrongness I feel now is separate from that. I reach out with my magic, but I don't sense anything.

"Does something feel wrong to you?" I ask Chai.

He shakes his head. "But then I'm about as blunt as a spoon when it comes to picking up on these things."

I knock on the door. No answer.

"Ilmu?" I call. "It's me, Apiya."

Still nothing. I knock again. I try to open the handle, but the door is locked.

"Stand aside," Chai says.

He gives a casual flick of his hand. The lock clicks, and the door opens.

"It's amazing you didn't turn burglar," I tell him as I go to step through.

Chai puts an arm out. "Too easy—I like the challenge of sculptures. And I go first."

I know better than to protest and follow him into the office. I frown as I enter. Ilmu normally inhabits one of the messiest offices I have ever seen—a veritable rat's nest of papers.

Now it's just an anonymous room. The ugly dark green metal desk in the middle of the room might be the same one she was using—it's hard to know. It was so covered in papers, it was hard to tell what colour it was. It's one of those desks with a partition along the front to keep the occupant's legs out of sight.

Behind the desk is the kind of metal chair we had in my classroom, at school. There's a filing cabinet to the left, but a few of the grey metal drawers gape open, clearly empty.

The room smells of dust and stale air, as if no one has been here for a long time. In fact, the only nod to this having ever been Ilmu's office is the small red shrine behind the desk. When I was last here, the shrine was dedicated to Wenchang Wang, the Chinese god of literature, but now the tiny statue, the incense holders, and the offerings are all gone.

"Could she have moved somewhere else?" Chai asks.

"I don't know. I'm not sure how easy or hard that is for a baku to do. I'm also wondering now if all the papers and all the stuff that used to be in her office were part of her glamour in some way... But then when I saw her at the temple her glamour didn't include papers and things."

We poke through the filing cabinet and the desk drawers, but they're all empty. There's absolutely nothing in the room to indicate anyone was here. I don't know what to make of it.

"We should go," Chai says. "There's nothing here."

I nod. I don't want to push my luck by asking him to stay longer. Before I head to the door, I glance around in one final sweep of the office. Something at the corner of my eye snags my attention and I turn to it. Something gleaming faintly on the floor, by one of the desk legs. The shadows kept it out of sight, but the edge sticks out just far enough to catch the light, which is what has caught my attention.

I crouch down to pick it up.

"What is it?" Chai asks.

"A piece of jade." I stand up, peering at it. "Maybe part of some kind of pendant or amulet?" The stone is pale green and polished, so that now that it's in the light, it shines. It looks like it was part of a larger piece, the rough edge to the right indicating where it was broken off.

"Well, you can look at that piece of jade at home from behind the safety of Mr Sangong's spells," Chai says. "No point taking any more risks than necessary."

I don't argue. Especially since it means I can finally clean up the mess back home.

~

CHAI DROPS ME OFF AT HOME AND THEN HEADS TO HIS STUDIO. I put the piece of jade aside and deal with the mess Hunter made. I'm not going to lie, it's a relief. Hunter is still clearly feeling very guilty, coming to me with his head low in apology.

Of course I've already forgiven him—who could stay angry at that little face? I give him a belly rub as a peace offering once the living room is once again clean.

Then I sit on the sofa and examine the broken piece of jade. At surface level, there's nothing particularly remarkable about it. It's a pretty piece of jade, unblemished by any lines or marks. The stone is smooth against my palm, faintly warm from where I handled it.

I reach for it with my magic. At first I just get a general sense of it, a sense of the spirit or essence of the jade, so to speak. It's sleek and cool and still. But this isn't just a piece of jade, it's part of something bigger, something that would have had its own essence.

Pushing deeper, I get a sense of memories. I can't see the memories, I can't sense them, but something about the jade is associated with them.

Which might indicate a link between the jade and Ilmu.

I concentrate harder, trying to get more from it, because I'm pretty sure I can sense the edges of something else. I frown and close my eyes, reaching as deep as I can. Whatever it is, I'm guessing at, it's just beyond my reach, as if I'm only just able to brush my fingertips against it but not grab it in my hand.

There—something. Something that feels like a bitter tang in the back of my throat. It's so faint, it's hard to focus on. I'm vaguely aware that I'm scrunching up my face in concentration as I keep reaching for that sensation.

There. A flash. Barely even that, but unmistakable. Distress.

It startles me into opening my eyes, breaking my connection to the jade. Ilmu's distress? Or someone else's?

I reach for it once more, but this time, no matter how hard I try, I can't get anything from the stone beyond the cool, smooth essence of the jade and the whiff of memories.

I could connect to the jade and nudge it, the way I do when I need to make a suggestion to an object, but I can't think of anything I could nudge it towards that would be helpful. I can't make the jade recreate the piece it was broken from, for example. That would be far too useful and powerful for my magic.

Eventually, I give up. I open my eyes and rub my thumb over the slick surface, feeling the rough, broken edge.

Distress.

If I wasn't already worried about Ilmu, now I definitely would be.

I place the jade on my coffee table and call Mr Sangong. When I get no reply, I send him a message asking about Ilmu and telling him she's not replying to her phone. I don't mention my trip to her office.

It's too early to be able to call my father and ask the fount of all obscure knowledge about the jade, so I send a message with a picture of the gemstone. Mum's back home now, and to everyone's relief, Dad made it through his time alone without starving or injuring himself.

Which also means that I can now send information to

Mum's phone, knowing that she'll show Dad. Makes life easier.

I haven't told them about Qinglong. In fact, I haven't told anyone but Chai, and not just because Mr Sangong told me to keep it to myself. I worry it would be upsetting for them to find out that their daughter was made from energy infused into a dead baby's corpse.

I mean, when you think about it, it's pretty creepy.

Sometimes I wonder about what Mr Sangong told me, about the fact that I will always carry death within me. A tiny—and crazy—part of me wants to reach inward to see if I can find it, this bit of death. But then with my luck that might mean I *actually* die or something like that. I've got enough going on at the moment.

If I hadn't seen into Mr Sangong's memories, I'd still think I was completely normal. I mean human—which until recently was my concept of normal. Nothing feels different, but then what do I know? I've never been human as it turns out, so I don't know what being human actually *feels* like.

Which if I stop to think about it for too long kind of screws with my head.

I also haven't made any other attempts to connect with Qinglong in any way. The ceremony back at the Akha village was too frightening and too painful. And who knows what the consequences of doing it again might be? Again, plenty of complications going on in my life as it is. No need to add to it.

Seriously, my life is such a disaster right now.

Which is why it would be great if I could do something to help Ilmu. Or at least check in on her. Do *something* useful. Make something right, instead of just sitting at home waiting, about as useful as a chocolate teapot.

Speaking of which...I go put on the kettle and open the metal tin containing my loose jasmin tea. I breathe in its floral smell. Tea always helps.

It's my British upbringing.

5

Once the tea is brewed, I decide to call Sarroch.

"What happened?" His voice is tight with worry as he answers his phone.

"Nothing has happened, I'm fine."

"Apiya, what have you done?" Now he sounds both annoyed *and* worried.

"Nothing. I haven't done anything. Geez, give me a break. I can't set foot outside of my house and no one can come in. Nothing is going on." I go a bit over the top with it —I'm a terrible liar.

But if I tell Sarroch that I went to Ilmu's office, he will freak, and that won't help anything. Also, I can't explain why it's so important that I check in on her without telling him about Qinglong and the whole 'I come from a dead baby infused with some qi that Qinglong stole from the world'.

"You've gone out, haven't you?" Sarroch asks accusingly. "You're out. Where are you? I'm coming to get you right now."

"You're mental. I'm *home*." Jesus—can weretigers smell lies over the phone or something?

"Right. Well then, you won't mind me coming over."

"Sure thing. Knock yourself out."

He wasn't lying. He arrives ten minutes later. I hear the screech of his tires—he drives similarly to Chai, which means scary fast.

My phone rings. I don't bother to pickup, opening the front door instead. Sarroch is just coming out of his car. The sun has already set, the golden light of late afternoon giving way to twilight.

"See? I'm home," I tell him.

Sarroch grunts. He looks over my shoulder, trying to peer into the house. Suspicious much? I mean, he's totally on the money—I *did* go out today, *and* Yue came to see me.

But of course I can't tell him about either of those things. I'll have to find a way to tell him about it all, and soon. Keeping secrets like this can so easily bite you in the ass.

I slip out without fully opening the door and close it behind me. Hunter will go mental if allowed out to go greet Sarroch, and I'm not sure right now is a time for his antics. Sarroch might like him, but it doesn't strike me as wise to let Hunter loose around an agitated weretiger.

Hunter paws at the door and whines. Sorry, buddy.

Sarroch leans against one of the pillars. Damn, he's handsome. Every time I think I've gotten used to it, it surprises me all over again.

"Apiya?"

"Huh?"

"I was asking what you were calling me about."

"Oh, right. Yeah." I hope I got away with the staring, otherwise that'll be pretty embarrassing. "Have you heard anything about Ilmu recently?"

"Ilmu? Why?"

"She's not replying to her phone."

"I wouldn't read too much into it, plenty of Mayak don't bother with mobile phones."

"I know, it's just that she used to be fine with hers. I could text her and everything. And I haven't heard from her since that Mustering I attended."

"That will be your answer, then. She's probably with the other baku, dealing with something related to Akiho—it would have been quite the crisis for them to have one of their own working with Nerong. They won't want to be disturbed."

"Hmm, maybe..." What he says makes sense, except for the broken piece of jade I found in Ilmu's office, and the distress I sensed from it. "Is there a link between the baku and gemstones?" I ask. "You know, like jade?"

"Jade? Why?"

"Not jade in particular. Any gemstone." I don't want to be obvious.

"I don't know. There might be. I'm not an expert on the baku."

"Do gemstones have any particular magical properties?"

"What is this about, Apiya?"

"Nothing, I'm just bored, and I'm worried about Ilmu. And I'm curious about the baku."

Sarroch sighs. "Okay. Sorry. I'm a bit jumpy tonight."

"Why, has something changed?"

Sarroch grimaces, an expression I've grown to learn means what has happened isn't great, and he doesn't want to tell me about it.

"Let me guess, you have been to see the Elders and things aren't going well?"

"Something like that."

And just like that, I get an idea for how to broach the subject of Yue with him. "Has it occurred to you that my situation could be greatly improved if you and Yue just got along a bit better? Then she might not be quite so eager to see my blood splattered on the wall."

Sarroch hangs his head and looks at the floor.

"She's sad," I say softly. "She's really heartbroken."

Sarroch grimaces again and runs a hand over his face. "I know," he mutters.

"She's probably feeling jealous of all the efforts you're making to try to keep me safe," I add, hoping I'm not pushing it too far. The only reason I know this is because she told me as much.

Luckily, Sarroch doesn't question what brought me to that conclusion.

"She probably is..." Sarroch sighs. He shakes his head. "But some things just can't be undone or unsaid."

"What things?"

"I was never averse to her and me having a close relationship. Friendship, caring, companionship, all those things were all fine. I just didn't feel for her like I did for Eyva, nor would I ever. And more to the point, I don't ever want to feel like that again. I will *never* take a mate again, that much I vowed. There are too many emotions wrapped up in that. Bonding, though, is a thing of ritual and magic, and doesn't require me to be emotionally involved. I would have happily shared that much of myself with her. But Yue couldn't accept that. Couldn't bear to come second to anyone. I forgave her when she tried to have someone use mind magic on me to get me to love her. I forgave all her attempts at trying to trick me into falling for her. And there were many. The spells, all the rubbish she wasted her time on. All of that I forgave in time because by then I knew I'd made a mistake both in bonding to Yue and in the way I'd handled her and the situation." Sarroch's eyes turn flat and icy blue, the colour of his tiger's eyes. "But I will never forgive her for attempting to have a baku consume my memories of Eyva." His voice is different, lower and more dangerous, with a soft rumble to it. "She's lucky I didn't kill her for that. So no, Yue and I will never get along. Ever. I tolerate her existence, only because to do otherwise would be a step back towards what I became after Eyva died."

I wince. Yue tried to remove his memories of Eyva? That's a low blow, even for her. It's also the death knell of me ever being able to fulfil the deal I made with her.

I glance over at Sarroch, but he's lost in thought. Night has settled, and in the dark something about him looks dangerous, primal. I must be picking up on his tiger.

Okay, so the possibility of making any progress with Sarroch that Yue might notice, even as far as friendship, has gone out of the window. Which means I need some other solution to the Yue problem.

Sarroch lets out a roar, moving at preternatural speed, startling me so badly that I yelp and jump back, slamming my back into my door.

The night has grown thick enough for Sarroch to be swallowed up by shadows, just beyond the light of the nearest streetlamp. There's an awful sound like crushing bones, following by pained grunting, and I can see two shapes moving in the darkness.

"Sarroch?" My voice sounds thin and scared. I have a hand on my door handle, ready to run in and lock it behind me. All the memories of Yue's attack come rushing back, the way my blood poured out of me, the awful terror at the thought I was going to die...

Sarroch reappears in the light a moment later, blood smeared over his cheek.

"What...what happened?" I ask. Behind him, the other

shadow has fallen still, slumped on the floor. "Did you kill him? Her?"

"No. Very few Mayak can die purely from physical wounds. We're made of magic, so magic needs to be involved to kill us. Although it will be a long and painful healing. Suitable punishment for being stupid enough to think he could slip past me and Sangong's spells." Sarroch's eyes are icy blue again.

"Who is it? Someone Yue sent?"

Sarroch shakes his head. He looks guilty. "This has to do with the discussion I've just had with the Elders. It's supposed to be confidential, but of course there are leaks."

I stay silent, waiting for him to say more. Maybe now he'll tell me what's going on.

"The discussion was about trying to get you a recognised status among the Mayak. You aren't Mayak, so you can't be recognised as such, but it seems you're not Touched, either. Which means you can't just be lumped in with them. It would be easy enough to 'classify' you as something other than the Touched, but I want you to be included beneath the Mayak umbrella, if that makes sense. Basically, so that a certain number of our laws apply to you—including the law that prevents Mayak from attacking other Mayak without a valid and sanctioned reason."

I already pretty much knew all of this, but I don't tell him so, in the hope that if I don't antagonise him, he might continue talking.

Something occurs to me, though. "Why didn't Yue face retribution for her attempts to get the pari-pari egg? The pari-pari were part of the Mayak." That was before they officially divorced themselves, because Yue attacked one of their eggs.

"The egg was unhatched. It wasn't considered Mayak back then."

"That's crazy. So if a female Mayak is pregnant, her baby isn't considered Mayak?"

"That's different—that kind of young is considered a Mayak. The problem with pari-pari eggs is that they're raw, uncrystallised magic. They aren't even pari-pari until they've hatched and have been guided to crystallise into a pari-pari. Until then they could crystallise into anything. So they can't be considered Mayak in egg form. If Yue had gone after a pari-pari youngling, the full weight of Mayak law would have fallen on her. But the egg falls outside of that."

"That is *seriously* warped."

Sarroch shrugs. "It is the way things are."

"So why is it so problematic for me to be granted the special status?"

Even before he speaks, I can tell he's about to feed me the line about not being able to share information.

"You said yourself there are leaks. Anything I know, I could have learnt from whatever it is who tried to come after me tonight. And if things are going bump in the night to try to get me, surely I have a right to know why."

Sarroch hesitates and then nods. "It's because of the precedent it would set. A human given any status above that of glorified cattle could eventually jeopardise the predators' ability to feed freely."

Predators like Yue.

"But if a human is allowed under the Mayak umbrella, then there are situations in which a human could be justified in killing other Mayak. And there is a worry that this would be a step towards ushering a new era in which humans who hunt and kill the Mayak return."

The humans who used to be able to do that, because

they drew magic from killing supernatural creatures, were apparently all slaughtered by Sarroch in revenge when they killed Eyva, his mate.

"I may have lost my temper and told the Elders that if I could go back in time, I would stop myself from slaughtering all those people. The Great Cleanse, they call it." Sarroch's voice is bitter. "I am considered a hero for having rid the world of that kind of human. It's bad enough that I have to live with my actions, it's worse when they get thrown at me as a reason for why there can be nothing to prevent Yue from killing you if she wants. Anyway, losing my temper only made things worse. I've been given an official warning."

Again guilt flashes on his features. "And that may have pushed one of the Elders against your cause." He sighs. "On top of which things have grown more complicated because it's all enmeshed in this issue of war with the Mundanes. The decision made about you is likely to influence the direction in which the Mayak turn on the war issue."

I know it doesn't change my situation, but knowing the ins and outs of what's going on behind the scenes helps a little. Even if what's going on isn't good news.

"Okay, so far I follow," I tell him. "So who is that creature over there?"

"No one important. Possibly sent by someone more important and more intelligent." Sarroch's expression turns grim. "Because of course if you die before this is resolved, that takes care of the problem. Anyone pro war or any predator would find it quite convenient if you stopped existing. And of course since for now you have no status within the Mayak, so long as you are killed discretely, there will be no consequences if anyone attacks you."

Great. Just great. That is exactly what I needed. More people who want me dead.

"I'm very sorry, Apiya. Just sit tight. I promise you, I will find a way to get you out of this predicament. I just need you to be patient and to stay home."

I nod. I definitely am not telling him about today's trip or about going to the Akha village. I look back into the night at the shape in the shadows. "What kind of creature is it?"

Sarroch shakes his head. "Dumb and strong. Nothing I can't handle."

Except that I can't expect Sarroch to be at my side for the rest of my life. I hesitate, as this next question is a bit delicate... "If physical blows can't kill Mayak, what about silver? How does that work exactly? Silver bullets can kill certain Mayak, right?" I keep it vague, especially since Sarroch is one of the creatures I know to be sensitive to silver.

I don't like guns—never have—but I'm starting to wonder if I might have to learn to shoot one and carry one with me.

"Silver has its own magic. As does iron, actually, although we weres aren't sensitive to iron magic. But even a silver bullet won't kill a weretiger. It can hurt us, slow us right down, cause all kinds of problems, but it still won't kill us. Not right away, at least. Over time, maybe, if not properly treated, and depending on where the wound is...A silver bullet shot by a person with magic, however..." Sarroch gives me a small smile. "I hope you're not looking for ways to be rid of me."

"Given that you just saved my life, that would be pretty ungrateful of me. No, it's more that I'm realising the vast depth of my ignorance when it comes to magic. I'm always playing catch up, always close to or completely out of my depth, but it's becoming clear that if I'm to survive in this world now, I need to know more than just the best way to barber people."

Sarroch nods. "That's wise. To be honest, I thought the Touched knew more about magic than they do."

I snort. "The Touched don't even really understand how it is that magic has Touched them. Or continues to Touch them. They know they have certain powers, they know how their powers work, and that's about it. The Mayak hold all the cards in that sense, and they don't share."

It's weird speaking of the Touched as 'they', but I definitely can't refer to them as 'us' anymore. I have a brief pang as I realise I no longer have people like me. I thought coming to Panong would mean I would find my people. Instead, what I found is that I have no people, and that no one is like me.

"Well, maybe once this is over we will see about remedying your lack of understanding. For now, I should go deal with this mess." Sarroch gestures with his chin at the shape in the shadow. The shape that is now slowly stirring.

My pulse starts to rise again. I never used to be so scared of things in the dark. And I definitely don't like the way that has changed.

"Sure. Nothing ends an evening like an attempted murder." I try for levity, but I'm not sure I've pulled it off.

Sarroch places a hand on the pillar nearest him. "Things *will* get better, Apiya. I promise you that. Please, just trust me. And magic help you, please stay inside your house until I have sorted it all out."

6

Once the door is securely locked, I put another pot of tea on. All that just happened definitely requires tea.

By the time I'm feeling the warmth of the teacup in my hand and breathing in the floral aroma of jasmine tea, I'm feeling better.

I still check all the doors and windows several times before going to sleep.

The following morning I wake up to two messages. One is from Mr Sangong telling me that Ilmu must be busy or that she might have forgotten about her phone, but that either way I shouldn't worry. A baku can handle herself.

I bite my lip. That's no help, and given the distress I felt in the broken jade, Ilmu might not be able to handle herself at the moment.

The other message is from Mum. Nothing on the piece of jade. Nothing on the link between jade and baku. She asks if it's important, because if so Dad will keep looking.

In short, no progress whatsoever on that front.

Last night it was a relief to have the safety of my spelled house, given that some nasty was after me in the dark.

Let's be honest. Last night I got dangerously closer to being cowardly, and I did some impressive cowering.

Thankfully, today I'm back to normal, which means hating how useless and helpless I've become. Ilmu might be in trouble but all I can do today is wait by the phone while I either clean my house again, or potter in my courtyard. Again.

I huff in frustration, throw my sheet back, and get out of bed. Hunter greets me happily. That's another thing. I can't even take my own damn dog for a walk—I've had to hire a walker instead or rely on Chai helping me out.

I miss taking Hunter to the park. I tell him as much as I stroke his ears, and then I head down to make tea.

"What's with the face?" Tim rubs himself against my legs.

"Good morning. It's lovely to see you too."

He jumps up in the kitchen counter, and I grab him and put him back on the floor.

"Spoilsport," he grumbles.

"I'm making breakfast. No furry creatures allowed on the kitchen counter."

"I'm not an *ordinary* furry creature, though."

"You have fur. Ergo, no climbing on the counter."

Tim begins to wash himself. "You didn't answer my question before. Why is it you look like a bulldog licking a stinging nettle?"

I snort, amused in spite of myself at the image. "Just...If I tell you something, will you keep it to yourself?"

"Who else would I tell?"

"I don't know—Mr Sangong?"

"He's busy these days. Haven't seen him in ages. The barbershop has been closed since you've been closeted in here."

I nod. I might be a fool for trusting a cat, but it's not like I have anyone else to talk to.

"I'm worried about Ilmu." I run Tim through finding the piece of jade as I make breakfast. It's a relief to share all of this with someone.

I've shared it with Chai, of course, but he doesn't really care. To him, this is just a source of potential risk to my safety.

Once my breakfast is made, I tend to Hunter's, and because I am a generous soul—*not* because Tim has me well-trained—I make Tim breakfast, too.

I finish explaining about the jade as I set Hunter's bowl down. He leaps on it with joyful abandon, inhaling the kibble and wet food mix so fast, he's *definitely* not tasting it.

Tim sits by his bowl, looks it over, and turns his nose up at it with an expression like what's in the bowl is cat vomit, not good quality cat food. Typical. I'm not making him something else, though.

He looks up at me. "Have you asked anyone else about the jade?"

"I tried. No link between jade and baku that Sarroch knows of—"

Tim makes a derisive noise. "What does *he* know?"

"Oh, I don't know. He's a powerful Mayak, so quite a lot, I would guess. I also asked my dad—"

"Why not ask Hunter while you're at it?" Tim asks. "Geez, some people. You have to spoon-feed them everything."

"You know something?"

"No. But I know that Meng Po is linked to memories, so she is likely to be knowledgeable about other creatures linked to memories. Like the baku."

Meng Po. Of course. She serves soup on the Bridge of Forgetfulness to souls who are about to reincarnate, so that they completely forget their past life. And she also runs a restaurant in town. Maybe she knows something about this broken piece of jade.

But I don't have her phone number, so that would mean leaving my house. Her restaurant is a Mayak space that's hidden in a parallel reality within a derelict building. In short, not the kind of establishment that has a phone number listed on Google.

"I can't leave the house on my own, though," I say aloud. "Especially not after last night. And I already know there's no way Chai will take me to Meng Po's."

"You won't be on your own," Tim replies smugly. "I'll be there."

"Not much of a reassurance."

"Did I, or didn't I stop Yue?" he asks archly.

"You did, but..."

"Well, then."

"Whatever attacked last night was apparently strong. According to Sarroch."

"Sarroch is only *part* feline," Tim replies contemptuously, as if that makes Sarroch inferior. Cats, I swear... "Anyway, I know how we can get to Meng Po's and back discretely. It'll be fine."

I'm not going to lie, I'm tempted. So tempted.

But it would be too much of a risk.

Tim doesn't hide his opinion of me not taking him up on his offer, spending the day communicating the kind of contempt I normally reserve for Justin Bieber's songs.

I do my best to ignore him, but my mind has other plans. It keeps going back to that sharp feeling of distress I picked up from the jade. Then there's the fact that the last time I saw Ilmu, she wouldn't acknowledge me. It was in Luyang temple, when Yue revealed she was the one who put Akiho, the unstable baku, in contact with Nerong.

Why did Ilmu not acknowledge me when I waved at her?

I scour my memory, trying to remember if Ilmu looked distressed or scared, or anything of the sort, but I wasn't really focused on her at the time.

I try to get back to my gardening for a while, but I find myself pulling out the broken piece of jade from my pocket every few minutes. It's like it's calling to me.

Ilmu got herself banished for me. That's also maybe why no one else cares that she's missing. Mr Sangong knows the truth, and isn't worried either, but then Mr Sangong is often incomprehensible in his reactions.

I return to the plant I'm repotting for no other reason than I need something to do.

Ilmu got herself banished for me. She has been banished for *years*. It's a huge sacrifice to make for someone.

And it has been a few weeks since I saw her at the temple. Plenty of time for things to go very wrong for her, if they weren't already wrong.

I glance over to where Tim is dozing in a patch of sun. "You said you have a way to go see Meng Po discretely."

"I do indeed, treacle," he mutters, not bothering to open his eyes. "But what does it matter, since you've decided to stick your head in the sand. I suppose I shouldn't be surprised. A part feline gave you an order, and humans are wired to obey felines."

That's not what makes my mind up to go. Not at all. I do *not* react to being baited by a cat.

I just can't keep sitting on my hands, knowing that Ilmu could be in trouble.

"Okay, then," I tell Tim. "If you promise that you have a way to help get to Meng Po and back safely, we'll go."

7

"You said you had a way to get us there *discretely*." I glare at Tim. We're standing just outside my front door, so still within the realm of Mr Sangong's protective spells.

"What? This is plenty discrete. Plus, it's the middle of the day, a time during which no Mayak in their right mind is going to come after you. Especially not with things as they are right now with the Mundanes."

"There is nothing discrete about my motorbike. And that's not *your* method of getting us there, that's *my* method of getting us there."

"Okay, firstly, you should know that when a human belongs to a cat, all their possessions also belong to the cat."

"I don't belong to you."

"Secondly, I'll be riding with you, and I have ways to make us unobtrusive, so relax."

I shake my head. "This is a terrible idea."

"It'll be fine, I tell you. Stop fussing. Anyway, it's not like you're drowning in other options."

The most annoying thing is that he's right. If I don't go

with him, I go back to my house and do nothing about Ilmu. Those are my two choices.

And right now the latter feels unacceptable.

So I slip on my helmet and get my bike off the centre stand. Tim jumps up on the tank, doing his bit of magic that means he won't slide off, no matter the bends I take.

I feel a faint tingle up my back, a buzzing in my hands.

"Is this your magic?" I ask the cat now happily curled up on my bike.

"Sure is. We're not invisible, but unremarkable. We'll make it to Meng Po without problems. You'll see."

And damn if he isn't right, which for once I'm happy about. I park outside the derelict building without seeing or sensing anything suspicious. So far, so good. I lock up my helmet and slip inside, Tim at my heels.

Majakai, Meng Po's restaurant, is hidden in true Mayak style. The host building is a dirty and abandoned shop-house in the heart of Old Town. The roof and walls remain standing, but that's about it. It's a shell of a building with plants growing through the roof tiles and an infestation of cockroaches inside.

I try not to tread on any of them as they skitter away from the disturbance of my heavy boots. I don't like to kill any animals, not even things like spiders and cockroaches. In fact, I'm quite fond of spiders—very intelligent, acrobatic animals, and I'm always in awe of their skill when I see them weave their web.

Tim trots behind me.

No one's waiting for me as I reach the metal door that marks the entrance to the restaurant. No Yue, no brutal minion waiting to attack me.

Maybe I'll carry out my errand and get home without any problems. Wouldn't that be something?

The door's handle is moist, as if the metal has been sweating in the heat. I grasp it and pause for a heartbeat, long enough to allow the security spells to pick up on my magic and allow me to transition through into the Mayak space beyond.

"I'll be back later," Tim says as soon as he steps in. "There's someone over there who loves me. *She* always gives me the *best* food." He gives me a look that implies 'unlike you' and trots off, ignoring me as I try to call him back.

I really shouldn't be surprised. The day Tim is reliably reliable, pigs will fly, hell will freeze over, and I'll be listening to Justin Bieber.

The restaurant is busy, as always. Day or night, the light never changes—a soft, golden shimmer that bathes everything in a warm glow. Slender columns reach up to the vaulted ceiling, creating a feeling not unlike a cathedral. Tall palms also reach up towards the ceiling, a collection of tiny fluttering lights weaving within their fronds. I have no idea whether those are tiny Mayak creatures—they might well be.

The tables are low and traditional, so that the guests have to sit cross-legged or on their heels to eat. That is other than the kappa lounging in small ponds, eating cucumbers or raw fish. I sweep a look around the room—no sign of Yue. And no one seems to be paying me any particular attention. Coast is apparently clear, for now.

A waitress approaches me as I remove my boots and place them on the shoe rack provided. She looks almost human, save for the exceptionally long, black eyebrows that curve over her temples, reaching up into her hair to merge with her complicated, coiled bun. She's wearing a hand-printed pakay, the traditional Panongian dress for women.

The pattern matches the beads dangling from the mother-of-pearl combs in her hair.

"I'm here to see Meng Po," I tell her. "I have something to ask her."

"Meng Po is busy," the waitress replies. "Would you like a table?"

"Could you please tell her it's important? I'm the protégée of Mr Sangong, and I'm also an associate of Sarroch's." The latter isn't technically true. Well, actually I don't know what I am to Sarroch, but I'm pretty sure he won't mind me using his name. I hope.

I'm not sure if it's Sarroch or Mr Sangong's name that does it, but the waitress asks me to wait as she quickly sashays away towards the kitchen. She returns a few moments later.

"This way."

Even though Meng Po is alone in the kitchen, there's a sense of bustle. Meng Po is old, very old. Her face is more seamed than a coal mine, and her hair is white as rice. Her eyebrows—also white—also reach up into her hair.

Same as the last time I saw her, she wears a very elaborate and cumbersome feiyu robe. It has a cross-collar opening that ties to the side of the waist with a ribbon, and more to the point, extremely wide sleeves that almost trail to the floor. Her impossibly long earlobes brush her shoulders, heavy-looking carved stone earrings dangling over her robe all the way to her breasts.

All around her, sauces bubble, woks sizzle as their contents fry, and bamboo steamers let out great clouds of steam. All of it is producing some seriously mouth-watering smells.

Meng Po stands in the middle of it all, serene, the flying fish pattern printed on the silk of her robe unmarred by any stains—she definitely doesn't cook her food by hand.

"You again," she tells me.

"Yes. You were right, by the way, I *am* an incarnated soul."

Meng Po nods once in acknowledgement, but doesn't ask me for any more information. That's a big thing among the Mayak—you never ask more about a person than that person is prepared to reveal to you of their own accord.

"I was hoping to ask you another question," I tell her.

"Tsk. You shouldn't keep digging around the past. It's not healthy. There's a reason I serve soup on the Bridge of Forgetfulness."

"No, it's not about me. It's about Ilmu. Do you know her? She's a baku."

Meng Po frowns, but she nods.

"I think she's missing. I found this, and I can sense an association to memories, so I thought maybe you could tell me what it's part of?" I show her the piece of jade.

Meng Po looks at it, then back up at me. "Where did you find it?"

"In Ilmu's office. Well, it's where I used to go to see her, anyway. Is the jade linked to her in some way? Or to the baku?"

"Why does it matter to you? You're human. This is Mayak business."

"Ilmu helped me a long time ago. I owe her. And she's missing. On top of which I got a sense of distress from the jade. If it's Ilmu's distress, I have to find out what happened to her and make sure she's okay."

Meng Po reaches into one of her huge sleeves and pulls out a pipe. It has a long, thin stem and a round bowl, and it's smoking, but there was no smoke coming out of her sleeve earlier, nor has it set her robe on fire—clearly a magical pipe. She sucks on it, regarding me.

"You're good at sensing things," she says.

"Yes. I can connect to the qi of things and people."

"Hmm."

Still she stares at me, puffing on the pipe. It suddenly occurs to me that she might know more about me than I previously thought, and Mr Sangong didn't want the truth of what I am to get out...

She might not know anything—I might just be worrying over nothing. And yet the way she looks at me...Like she's evaluating me.

"Can you tell me about the piece of jade?" I ask, to stop my mind from going in circles over what she might or might not know.

"It's part of a key."

"A key to what?"

"The baku's domain. But if it's broken, then someone must have been forced through."

"Forced?"

Meng Po nods.

Well, that matches the distress I sensed. Something must have happened to Ilmu. "What do I do? How can I help her?"

"You can't help her. This is baku business. Not yours to meddle with."

"I'm not standing by and doing nothing if Ilmu's in trouble."

Meng Po shrugs. "Tragedies happen all the time and you do just that—stand by and do nothing."

"But this is different, because I know about it, and because Ilmu is my friend."

"Well, then. Go and do something about it."

"Can't you help me? Or at least point me in the right direction?"

"If you could do something about it, you wouldn't need my help. This isn't your business, girl. So leave it be."

Meng Po turns away, dismissing me. I open my mouth to argue, but the waitress—who I'd completely forgotten about until now—touches my arm and shakes her head.

I'm still rational enough to know it's probably not wise to go antagonising someone as old and powerful and Meng Po, but damn it's hard to turn away and follow the waitress out.

"Seriously, does no one care about Ilmu?" I mutter under my breath as the waitress leads me back to the door. Apparently not. Everyone has told me to leave her to it, but I can't do that.

If she has been forced into the baku's domain, that begs the question of who forced her and why? And if they forced her, what else are they doing to her?

"Thank you for coming by," the waitress tells me, startling me out of my thoughts.

I shake my head. "I achieved nothing other than confirming that Ilmu is in some kind of trouble," I reply. "I'm really not sure coming here was a good idea at all." I don't mention the risk I took in coming.

I'm putting on my boots when the waitress reaches down and hands me an incense stick.

I frown, taking it. "What's that?"

"It's to help you see those who are no longer in this world. Often it's used for the deceased, but if Ilmu is in the baku's domain, then she's no longer in this world. Light it at night, think of her, and you'll see her in the incense smoke."

I feel a rush of gratitude. "Thank you."

"Just don't tell anyone I gave you this. Not everyone is indifferent to what's going on with Ilmu."

"You know what's going on with her?"

"No. Until you came in today, I didn't even know she was missing. But I always liked her, and I was sorry to see her get banished. She didn't even complain when I had to turn her away. Normally those who get banished are furious, but she was very accepting of her fate."

Which only makes me feel worse that this punishment was brought on because she helped me.

I thank the waitress and hurry out.

OF COURSE, TIM IS NOWHERE TO BE FOUND, SO I HAVE TO GO home alone. I'm tense for the whole ride back, my senses straining, half expecting someone to jump me.

But it's a bright afternoon, and no one even looks in my direction. I make it home without any problems. No one's waiting for me at my house, either.

Given last night, I know I'm not being paranoid, but from what Tim says, maybe daytime *is* safe for me to go out, and it's only at night I need to be locked at home. I'm not sure it's worth testing that theory out, though.

I wait impatiently for night to fall so I can light the incense. I have it set up in my incense holder, a long, narrow piece of carved wood. The stick is slotted into the hole made for that purpose, so the tip hovers at a forty-five degree angle above the wooden dish.

I swear time has never moved so slowly, but finally the sun has set and the night has settled.

I strike a match and present it to the incense while picturing Ilmu in my mind's eye. Smoke begins to coil up at once. I stare at it, still thinking of Ilmu.

The smoke grows a little thicker, and then it fans out.

Within that space it starts to curl and swirl, creating shapes, making it impossible for me to see past it. There's way too much smoke given how slender the stick is, so there's clearly magic at work.

And then the smoke parts, but instead of my living room, the space within the smoke reveals another room. All I can see is a row of dark green bamboo that have been stripped of their leaves, leaving only the vertical poles. Ilmu is sitting against them. She's in her true form, with the head of an elephant, the body of a bear, and the legs of a tiger.

Because she's in true form, I can't read her facial expression, but her body language is very clear. She's scared, or in pain—something wrong, whatever it is.

I hesitate, unsure if the incense allows me to communicate—the waitress said nothing about that. I'm also unsure whether that would be a good idea. Someone might be out of sight, someone who would hear.

Ilmu looks up suddenly and catches sight of me. Her eyes widen.

And then another face comes into view. The woman is pale, and she looks like she has just risen from a bath, water running off her face and neck. Her black hair is long, plastered to the sides of her face, disappearing beyond the limits of the smoke opening.

She too looks straight at me, as if she can see me. Is she being held prisoner with Ilmu? The woman's expression turns to one of distress.

"Where are you?" I ask her. "How can I get to you to help?"

The woman lets out an earsplitting screech. Her eyes have turned slitted and yellow like that of a snake, her open mouth revealing a forked tongue.

Something about the scream causes my body to freeze up completely.

Which is why when her hand reaches out of the smoke for me, I can't move. Nor can I move when her hand grabs my arm.

Hunter is barking like crazy. Still I can't move.

I have time to think "Shit" before she drags me into the smoke.

8

I come to, discovering a horridly bitter and furry taste in my mouth. I try to move and groan as my entire body feels like it's been slammed into by a bus. My eyelids are gummed together, and I have to peel them slowly, painfully open.

Error. The light is like needles stabbing through the jelly of my eyes, straight into my brain. I wince and squeeze them shut again, my breath whistling noisily in and out of my nose.

At least it's cool, even a little chilly. I don't think I could stomach heat right now.

"You're the first human to transition to our realm, so it's probably taking your body time to adjust."

I let out a muffled sound of protest and carefully peel an eyelid open again to see who's been speaking to me.

"Ilmu," I croak. "Thank god. I was worried... I wanted to help you."

She's wearing her human glamour, and she shakes her head. "You're an idiot, Apiya. You can't help me, and now you've got yourself into a very dangerous position."

I open both eyes again, groaning briefly at the pain from the light. As my eyes adjust, I can start to look around me. We're in the room I saw through the incense smoke. The walls are made from tight rows of large, dark green bamboo, and there's a single, sliding door made of lattices of black lacquered wood over which is stretched pale rice paper.

At first I think we're in some kind of outer courtyard, but when I look up, I see a bamboo ceiling.

I push myself up slowly to sit. The floor is covered in tatami mats, their springiness making lying on the floor quite comfortable. The bamboo poles, or maybe the tatami mats, give off a faint grassy smell.

"I had to do something," I tell Ilmu. "I found out what you did for me—"

"Shhh." Her eyes grow wide, darting around us. "Never speak of it," she whispers. "*Especially* not here."

"Why? Where are we?"

"In the realm of my kind."

"The baku?"

"Yes."

I nod. So Meng Po was right. "Is that why in your true form you don't have all the records around you? I saw you through the incense smoke before."

Ilmu nods. "Our knowledge is stored differently here."

"Have you been here all this time? I've been trying to get in touch with you since the day at the Luyang Temple, but..."

"Yes, I've been kept here. It goes without saying that things like mobile phones don't work out here, even if I had one with me."

"Why have they been keeping you here? Are you a prisoner?" I shift until I'm also sitting against the bamboo. The blood is returning to my limbs—I must have cut circulation by lying awkwardly on them—making them tingle and itch. I'm finally starting to feel like an approximation of a human.

"If by prisoner you mean I don't want to be here, then yes," Ilmu replies. "After everything that happened with Akiho, they decided they wanted to revisit the memories that got me banished, because everyone agreed the memories must belong to an ancient Mayak. Everyone has been trying to establish who this Mayak could be by looking through my memories, but so far they haven't managed to figure it out. And of course I haven't told them—" Ilmu freezes, listening. She grips my arm, leaning towards me and whispering urgently. "Do not tell them anything about what you are. *Nothing.*"

Before I can ask more about that, the rice paper door slides open silently. I recognise the woman standing in the doorway. She was at the last Mustering at the Luyang Temple. She was also the one who explained what they had discovered about Akiho, so she must be a kind of leader for the baku. And she still looks like a librarian.

But whereas I normally associate librarians with friendly, helpful people, her face behind her glasses is pinched with displeasure, made all the more severe by her poker straight, shoulder length black hair that frames her face.

She's wearing a cardigan the colour of oatmeal over a white shirt and a long brown corduroy skirt—a good choice given the chilly temperatures. My own bare arms are sprouting goosebumps. I'm only wearing ripped denim shorts and a cropped tank top. At least I have my heavy boots, keeping my feet warm.

"Ah, you're awake. We need to ask you some questions," she said.

Ilmu drops her human glamour, bowing her head low in

her true form. "Please don't consume her memories. She is nothing more than a friend who was worried about my absence."

"Well, this friend of yours managed to enter our realm without our permission, so we need to know how she did that."

"I'm very happy to explain," I say quickly, horrified at the thought of any of my memories being consumed.

It's one thing for Ilmu to have done that in order to help keep me alive back before I was 'born'. Even though I was already born.

This is too confusing to think about.

It was 'before', so I can make my peace with it. I am absolutely not prepared to have any memories consumed now.

"And how else are we going to know whether you are telling us the truth or not?" the librarian asks.

"What do you mean?"

"I mean, I need to see your memories to know whether you are speaking the truth."

"You can look without consuming," Ilmu suggests deferentially.

The librarian frowns at her. "I didn't ask for your advice." She turns to me. "If you would follow me. Please."

I push myself to standing and fall into a fighting stance despite my body's protests. "I'm not going anywhere until you promise that you're not consuming my memories. And trust me when I tell you that I'm a very good fighter." Well, without my razors or any other weapon, I'm probably very outmatched against a magical creature, but a little bravado can't hurt. The baku are supposed to be quite gentle, after all.

The librarian sighs, looking unimpressed. She steps

aside to free up the doorway, and she calls out some words in a language I don't understand.

The woman I saw in the incense smoke appears in the doorway. Except that she's not a woman at all. She has the head, chest and arms of a woman, and she still looks dripping wet, as if she has just come out of the ocean.

The rest of her, however, is an enormous snake covered in iridescent blue and green scales. Her black hair is incredibly long, more than two yards long, maybe even three. It's wet and plastered all the way along her body. Her eyes are yellow and slitted and the forked tongue I saw before darts out quickly, tasting the air.

Nure onna. A kind of coastal, water-dwelling vampire. She slithers fully into the room. Her snake body is huge. It coils up until it's blocking most of the room's entrance. She uses it to keep her human-looking part raised up well over six feet in height.

She opens her mouth, no doubt to screech again. I don't give her the time. If her top half looks human, it should be prey to the same vulnerabilities. I jump forward and swing my leg around in a kick that hits her straight in the solar plexus.

With my heavy boots, that's going to hurt.

And yet, it's not enough to send her crashing back— she's too firmly planted with that enormous snake body. But it does wind her, stopping her from screeching.

She straightens herself, yellow eyes flashing. I'm expecting an attack, but I'm not expecting her hair.

It darts away from her body as if animated of its own will and lashes towards me.

I block with my left arm, grabbing a handful of it. It's wet and slick, almost as slimy as seaweed. It tightens itself around my arm. I guess the legends that the nure onna catch humans with their hair and drag them into the sea to drown them before they drain them of their blood are correct.

More of the nure onna's hair lashes towards me, but I'm only able to catch part of it with my right hand. If only I had my razors.

The rest of her hair wraps itself around my throat. She's not strangling me, but her hold is tight enough to be uncomfortable, bordering on painful. Her hair is also so long that I'm well out of reach from kicking her anywhere that would be vulnerable enough to feel the impact.

I still let out a couple of kicks, as powerful as I can make them, but the impact of my boot against her snake body feels a little like me kicking a dense punching bag, and it clearly has no effect on her.

Keeping me trapped with her hair, the nure onna begins to slither out the door, and I have no option but to get dragged along with her.

9

I'm brought to a room that is so staggering, for a moment I forget my predicament and gawk. In a way, it's like a large-scale version of the bamboo slat library I normally see around Ilmu in her natural form. And yet, it's so much more than that.

The ceiling arches impossibly high overhead, a delicate network of wooden beams that cross each other like a more complex version of the skeleton of a traditional Japanese paper umbrella.

The room is circular and all along the walls are innumerable bamboo slats, some gathered and tied with a red ribbon, keeping their contents hidden, others dangling freely, the tiny black symbols etched upon their surfaces visible. One section houses what looks like slender wooden paddles also engraved with yet more symbols.

I have no concept of what these symbols represent and just how much knowledge and how many memories are contained in each record, but the room feels ancient, like it was standing before time began.

There's a sense of worlds within worlds within worlds. Of the vastness of the memories contained.

I don't often use the word awesome, but something about this room, simply furnished as it is, creates a real sense of awe.

Green orbs float a little bit higher than head height, diffusing a soft green light beneath them.

The librarian walks over to a low table, gracefully lowering herself to sit on her heels.

"Please take a seat." It's not an invitation but a command.

Not that I have much of a choice. The nure onna unceremoniously dumps me on the floor next to the table, her hair releasing me abruptly. I cough a couple of times and run my fingers along my throat to check for any cuts, but other than feeling a bit bruised and a bit damp, I'm fine.

I glare at the creature before sitting cross-legged at the table. There's obviously no point resisting.

"I need to know how you were able to enter our domain," the librarian says.

Her human glamour shimmers and disappears, leaving me facing another baku in true form. She's larger than Ilmu, and the markings on her body are different, the tiger stripes of her leg reaching up past her shoulders before blending into the bear-like part of her body.

Where Ilmu looks shy and retiring in her true form, the librarian looks powerful and not particularly friendly. And she's big enough that she probably could easily do me quite a lot of damage, if she felt so inclined.

"So. Tell me." Her voice is deep, too deep for a woman. I suppose the acoustic of that larger rib cage is bound to have an impact on her voice.

"I was given incense by one of Meng Po's waitresses," I tell her quickly. "She said it would enable me to see people who are no longer in our world. She told me to light the incense and think of the person I wanted to see, and I would see them. It worked, but then the nure onna appeared, reached out of the smoke, and pulled me in."

The librarian's head snaps sideways, glaring at the nure onna. The librarian lets out a few angry, guttural words. The nure onna shakes her head and replies something, then she turns and slithers out of the room.

"We will see if you speak the truth," the librarian says, switching back to Panongian.

I feel a sharp spike of terror. "Don't consume my memories." I'm not too proud to beg, not if it will save my memories.

The baku have never seemed like scary creatures before, but right now I'd rather face Yue.

The librarian cocks her head, her large eyes regarding me. "Remember how you came here. And be aware that I can tell the difference between a true memory and a fake mental picture. If you attempt to trick me, I will devour a lot more than the memories of how you came to be here."

I shake my head. "Surely there must be another way."

"Remember!" Her voice booms, echoing in the large space, making me jump.

I swallow around the hard lump that has formed in my throat. The baku's eyes are cold and dark within the elephant skin of her head.

Not wanting her to carry out her threat to devour more than the memory of how I came here, I close my eyes and remember. I remember how the waitress gave me the incense, how she told me to think of Ilmu. Then I remember being at my house, and lighting the incense stick. The way the smoke coiled and then parted to reveal Ilmu.

And then how the nure onna grabbed me, followed by

the spike of panic when I realised she was bringing me into the smoke.

As I remember, it's like white space is following every memory. As I remember, I'm aware of it disappearing behind me, so I can't then look back to remember again. The memory is just... gone.

I open my eyes and gape at the librarian. I no longer have any clue of how I came to be here. I can remember waking up in Ilmu's room, clear as day, and I can remember deciding to go to see Meng Po with Tim. But the rest is... gone. Not unclear, not vaguely there. Just...gone.

"Hmm, so you told the truth."

"Can you return my memories to me?" I ask. "Aren't baku able to regurgitate memories?" I don't mention that Ilmu told me this in case it gets her in trouble.

"Quiet, or I will remove your memory of me consuming your memories so you will have no idea how they came to disappear."

I gulp, keeping silent. My heart is pounding hard as the sheer power of a baku becomes horribly real. If she wants, she can wipe the slate clean. She could consume the memories I have of my parents, of Hunter, of Chai, of my house. She could leave me a complete amnesiac with no idea of who I am. And she doesn't even have to touch me.

The nure onna returns then, followed by a slightly smaller one. To my untrained eye they look identical, down to their features, their slitted eyes and serpentine bodies, but the smaller one is hanging her head in a way that communicates shame or contrition.

The librarian lets out a stream of angry words and the contrite nure onna cringes. She replies, keeping her eyes trained on the floor.

The librarian makes a sound of disgust and waves her

trunk, dismissing them both. The larger nure onna grabs a fistful of hair from the smaller one, making her wail. Then they slither out together.

"Younglings." The librarian shakes her head and turns back to me. I'm not going to lie, I also feel like cringing under her stare. "Thank you for speaking the truth. Not only did what you say match your memories, but it also matched what the nure onna reported. I don't know why she thought you smelt interesting..." The librarian pauses and considers me. "How did you meet Ilmu?" she asks. "You will show me, in your memories."

"Can you just look at my memories without consuming them?"

"You can either bring up the memories of how you met Ilmu, or I can go searching for them, but that means I will consume a great deal more."

My mouth goes paper-dry with panic. "Okay, Okay, wait. Just... Give me a moment. It's hard to think right now. Just... let me get my thoughts organised."

All the moisture from my mouth seems to have relocated to my palms, which are sweating heavily. I wipe them on my shorts.

I need to be smart about this. Ilmu told me not to say anything about what I am, and given what the librarian is like, I am most definitely heeding that warning. Anyway, I have no memory of that very first, long ago meeting.

What I think of as meeting Ilmu is the first time I went to see her in her office.

But I still need to be careful. Make sure I bring up memories that will make it look like how we met was completely innocent.

"Okay, I'm ready." I take a deep breath and bring up the first memory.

I feel my gut twist inside me at the knowledge that it will be consumed. I show the librarian my father as a professor in Panong University. Just one instance of seeing him in his office.

The awful white space from before follows the memory, wiping it out until I no longer know what I have just brought up. I continue forward, hoping I didn't show anything too important.

I show the librarian me moving to Panong and not knowing anyone, followed by one of the many nights when I felt lonely and homesick. There were many of those.

Then I show her a part of the conversation with my father where he tells me about Ilmu, followed by me going to Ilmu's office at the University.

By the time we're done, I know that I showed the librarian memories about how I met Ilmu, but I have absolutely no idea what that was. I have nothing left about our first meeting. I just know that I know her.

Not knowing the memories I've lost is terrifying. I know I have lost something but I don't know what exactly. The one thing I cling to is that I know I had a plan for what to show the librarian, but I have no way of knowing if she took more than I wanted her to.

"Hmm, very good." The librarian's eyes flutter as she turns her gaze inward. Then her eyes snap back to me. "I'll have you escorted back to Ilmu's room. I will have to decide what to do with you later."

10

B ack in Ilmu's room, I move slowly, like a zombie. I can feel the loss of my memories weighing heavy within me—an awfully blank, leaden space. The fact that I don't know what I've lost makes it worse, somehow. It leaves my imagination free to make the nebulous feeling huge and painful. What if I accidentally gave up a precious memory, because it popped up unexpectedly? What if I've now forgotten something important about my parents?

"Are you okay?" Ilmu asks. She's wearing her human glamour again, and she puts a finger to her lips as I reach her side, then touches her ear. Someone's listening—got it.

I nod and sit next to her, drawing my knees up to my chest for comfort. I can't help returning to that blank space inside me over and over again, like worrying a loose tooth.

What have I lost? What if the librarian took more than what I selected? What if I selected what I thought was unimportant, but that will one day turn out to be hugely significant?

Ilmu gestures for me to come closer. She puts a hand on my arm, and I suddenly feel a pressure build in my ears as if we're on a plane that's going high up in the sky.

"Okay," Ilmu whispers. "We can talk. So long as we keep it quiet, no one should be able to hear. Tell me what happened."

"She wanted to know how I came here and how we met. She had me bring up memories of both things." I shake my head. "I don't know what she took, but I know there's a blank space inside me. I can feel the loss."

Ilmu nods. "It's very unsettling at first. Your subconscious is a lot smarter than your conscious self, and it can tell the difference between a memory gap and a hole from memories being consumed. That's why it feels so weird. We can make a human's subconscious bury memories—people do that all the time. That's far less unsettling—it feels no different to forgetting something. But the problem is that those memories can eventually be called back."

"I'll never get back what I lost?"

Ilmu shakes her head. "I'm sorry." She hesitates. "Did you show her the *very* first time we met?" she whispers so low I barely hear her.

The emphasis she put on the word 'very' makes it clear that she's referring to the time Mr Sangong asked her to devour all my memories as a baby so I would no longer remember that I was made by Qinglong.

"I don't know what I showed her," I whisper back. "I don't remember the very first time we met, just what I was told about it, and if I still remember that, then I guess I can't have shown her."

"You're right. And anyway, if you had, she wouldn't have brought you back here."

"What's going on, Ilmu? Why are you here? Why would it be so bad for her to know what I am?"

Ilmu sags and leans back against the bamboo wall. "I won't ask you how you came to discover what you are. I'd rather not know. But after everything that happened with Akiho, the baku decided they needed to revisit my acquired memories that seem to belong to an old and powerful Mayak. A Mayak would have to be very powerful to have memories of Qinglong. Normally such a Mayak's memories would only be absorbed near death, but there hasn't been the death of a powerful Mayak recently. I mean in the last few decades. And I wouldn't show evidence to confirm that the memories were absorbed with full consent and according to our rules. Normally a baku would first store a memory of the Mayak in question giving their consent. Since I didn't have that, I was banished.

"Chizu and the others forced me to come back here so they could go through my memories to try to figure out who they belong to, in order to check the situation out. Make sure everything was above board and if not, make reparations."

Ilmu looks away. "Being forced into the baku realm and then being forced to submit to a search of your memories for long periods of time is...painful. It's a violation. It's like..." Her whole body shudders with revulsion. "Like clawed fingers scratching your soul. Like glass in your mind. If that glass was tainted and foul."

"Ilmu, I'm so sorry."

"There's no need for you to apologise—this isn't your fault. We baku are normally a peaceful kind. But things these days things are so...complicated. Out of kilter." She shakes her head. "It's having all kinds of consequences. Not that long ago, the baku would never have forced one of their own to submit to that kind of treatment."

"God, I feel awful. If you hadn't—"

"Don't speak of the past. Especially not here. Anyway, everyone gave up—or rather I think Chizu dismissed them all."

"Chizu—that's the librarian?"

Ilmu raises an eyebrow. "Librarian? I wish she was that harmless. She's the most powerful of us all. But yes, it's her. She continued looking through my memories. I'm not sure how, but she managed to figure out that the memories belong to Qinglong's created daughter, and from that surmised that the energy has been hidden on earth somewhere. I had already purged myself of the memories of you as a baby and Mr Sangong telling me his plan for you."

"But shouldn't that mean that you should no longer know about it?"

"Purging doesn't work in the way Chizu consumed your memories. A baku can control and manipulate their own memories far more subtly. I purged the actual memory but not the knowledge. I can't bring up the visuals, but I *know* what happened. I thought I had effectively erased all clues that could lead back to you, but I clearly left something behind."

"But why is that so bad? What's so dangerous about Chizu knowing about me?"

"The baku are as divided about the human issue as the rest of the Mayak. Chizu is pro war, for example. The majority of us are still for peaceful cohabitation, and that is putting us out of favour with certain powerful Mayak. This business with Akiho hasn't helped, putting us out of favour with peace -favouring Mayak as well.

"I think Chizu hopes that if she can find the being whose

memories I ingested, she can turn this to the baku's advantage. That's what she says at least, but I'm pretty sure she's hoping to work it to her own advantage. That's why she dismissed the others. She's ambitious, and securing something like this would give her quite the leg up in Mayak society. If she's able to break the stalemate of the Mundane problem, that would establish her as a power."

"Wait, I'm confused. How would knowing about me break the stalemate?"

Ilmu gives me a sad smile. "Since Qinglong made her daughter from pure qi, the being could be essentially dismembered, the container discarded, the energy used to create something that could assist the Mayak in their situation with the Mundanes." Ilmu's eyes darken as she looks at me. "Destroy the being in order to turn it into a weapon that could help subjugate humanity. In essence, do what Yue was trying to achieve back when she went after the unhatched pari-pari egg, except with raw energy instead of raw magic. It's just as corrupt, though. Just as awful. That energy *was* stolen, which was a crime. But to weaponise it would be a greater crime and only push things further out of alignment."

I've grown very still at the mention of dismemberment. Can they do that? Can the Mayak really take me apart like I'm just a piece of IKEA furniture, use the parts they want and discard the rest?

"When you say 'discard the container'..."

"I mean your body, which currently serves as a container for the energy."

I'm suddenly left facing one of life's big philosophical questions. "But without my body...Would I still be me? Can I still exist without it?"

Ilmu sighs. "I don't think so. There will be too much link

between your memories and your body. Same for your personality. Destroy the physical and the concept of Apiya will also be destroyed."

The concept of Apiya. I don't think I ever felt like less of a person.

"So what would be left?"

"Raw energy."

"But is it...Would it still be sentient? Conscious? Would I be a different version of myself?"

"I suppose it must be sentient, since it was sentient before it was infused into the baby. But it's hard to know what it would be like after a trauma such as having its host destroyed. And in any case, that wouldn't matter, because the idea wouldn't be to simply let that energy be, but to turn it into a weapon, and to do that, it would either stop being sentient, or become sufficiently mindless to be virtually non-sentient."

"The only obstacle left," Ilmu continues in a low voice, "Is the fact that Chizu doesn't know what creature the energy was hidden in. That's what she's looking for. But she doesn't know who hid the energy, and she's looking for someone with a lot of power."

Thank god for my crappy, weak magic, I guess. And I'm guessing the fact that I'm human has thrown Chizu off, making her overlook the young nure onna's interest in me.

I remember Sarroch explaining that there are no consequences for Yue going after a pari-pari egg because it's not considered part of the Mayak. It would be the same with me, even if the Mayak knew the truth of what I am.

That must be why Mr Sangong doesn't want anyone to know what I am. The moment they know, how many would want to do the same as Chizu? If it would break the stalemate and ensure a Mayak victory over Mundanes, I'm sure many would be happy to throw ethics out of the window. If ethics even come into play—because I'm not Mayak at the end of the day.

I have no idea how many Mayak are only in favour for peace because they believe the war against Mundanes can't be won. I could be the missing element that swings the tide of opinion.

"Jesus," I say at last. My situation is looking seriously screwed up. And seriously dangerous. "We need to get out of here."

Ilmu raises an eyebrow. "Way to state the obvious, Captain Evident."

A ghost of a smile flits across my lips. It's nice to see Ilmu's sarcasm make an appearance. It cheers me up just a tiny fraction. "I'm guessing you don't know how to get out of here or you would have been gone by now."

She frowns at me like I'm an idiot. "Of course I know how to get out of here. I'm in my own kind's realm. What's keeping me here is that if I leave without Chizu's permission, she has threatened to report me as unstable. And unstable baku aren't normally allowed to live very long."

"Can she do that? Surely she can't unilaterally declare you unstable without someone else confirming that?"

"She could use the memories of you that I ingested, arguing that I took them without consent, and that this was the start of my instability. She might still do that if she doesn't find you."

I nod, understanding. "Because the only way to counter her accusation would be for the person whose memories these are to come forward and confirm that consent was given. Which would then mean she knows who Qinglong's daughter is."

"Exactly."

Ilmu is in as bad a spot as I am, really. I make a decision. "I'm going to get out of here somehow and talk to Mr Sangong and Sarroch about this, to see if some way out can be found. They're trying to get me an official status among the Mayak. The moment they achieve that in such a way that I'm properly recognised as a member of the Mayak, then I can go public with what I am and Chizu's threats go away. All of it goes away."

I pause as something occurs to me. "Why have you been helping me all this time? You could have given me up right away and saved yourself all that pain, not to mention the danger of Chizu's threats."

"Easy, don't get ahead of yourself. I'm not doing it for you, rather for what you represent if Chizu has her own way."

"You mean the war with and subjugation of Mundanes? Do you really care that much about us humans?"

"It's not a matter of me caring about humans. It's a matter of what the magic needs. The magic was created, was *designed* on the basis of humans and Mayak coexisting within it. It's like with nature and wildlife. If you took every single wild animal and put them all in zoos, the natural world wouldn't work. Trees and numerous plants couldn't reproduce properly, so the forests would end up collapsing, and with them the planet's ability to process carbon dioxide. Likewise, if you took all the insects away. They're such an essential part of the world we exist in, that none of us— magical or Mundane—could survive without insects. They break down dead matter, create soil, pollinate plants to produce the food we eat...Without them the world would starve while drowning in dead things. And yet very few people think that insects matter. Humans are the same."

"Humans are the same as insects?" I ask dryly.

"Yes. Small, insignificant, and in numbers to rival insects." There's no humour in Ilmu's tone. She's dead serious. "And yet I believe they are essential to the balance of the magic. Not everyone agrees with this, but I am firmly of the opinion that if humans are fully subjugated and brought under Mayak control, the magic will cease to be stable. Mr Sangong is right—we have to find a way to coexist peacefully. If humans destroy us, the magic will fall into chaos, and it will destroy them. But if we subjugate humans, or worse, destroy them, the magic will do the same to us."

"But weren't humans once under Mayak control? Long ago?"

"Mundanes were never under Mayak control. We just all lived peacefully, even though we Mayak were so much more powerful. The Mundanes came to worship many of us, but they did that of their own accord, not because they were controlled, or otherwise enslaved."

"What about the humans who were able to draw magic from Mundanes? The ones Sarroch killed?" I'm still very curious about those, and if there's any link between them and the Touched.

"He told you about that, did he? The Great Cleanse. Look at the events of our history. A human specie disappears, and then slowly the Mundanes turn away from the Mayak. The balance that existed between us starts to gradually wear down. Again, not everyone agrees with me. But I believe Sarroch's actions set off a slow chain reaction that brought us all the way here."

"I thought it was Qinglong stealing qi from the world?"

"What do you think caused her to do that?" Ilmu sighs. "The magic works in mysterious ways. It is like the most complex of webs, touching, affecting everything. It's the very fabric of life. It's what brought the first spark of life to the primordial ooze that we all descend from. No one can ever hope to understand the full depths of its complexities or the infinite consequences a change can bring. One thing is for sure, though—magic requires balance. Without it, we are all lost. And the path Chizu is in favour of taking seems, to me, the best way to push us further in the direction we are already headed. Which is away from balance, away from peace, and towards destruction."

She falls silent and I mull over all she has just told me. I feel like the last few weeks have taught me more about magic, the Mayak, the Mundanes, than all the years I've spent in Panong. And I'm starting to realise the full scale of my ignorance.

A question rises up sharply within me. What is Mr Sangong's motivation for me figuring out what I am? His *true* motivation? He wanted me to remember what I was. Why? He never said anything about the fact there would be those who would want to take me apart, but he must have known that was a possibility.

Why then would he want me to remember when that would only increase the risk of word of my true nature getting out? Why push me into difficult positions in the hope my true nature would come back to me?

"I need to get out of here now." All of a sudden I feel really agitated. I need to get back home, and...Will I be safe at home? Truly safe? Mr Sangong set the spells that protect me from others. But if I can't truly trust his motives...

"Not yet," Ilmu replies. "The tides aren't right."

"Tides?"

"Yes, our realm is connected to the coast. That's why we have the nure onna to help us guard its entrance. When the tides are high enough, that's when they go out to feed. They won't all go, of course, but there should be less of them, which will make moving about easier."

I try not to think about the fact that the nure onna feeding no doubt involves some humans being tangled in their hair, drowned, and drained of their blood.

11

———

I don't know how Ilmu can tell when the tide is high, given that there are no windows, no link to the outside world. And yet a couple of hours later she gestures silently for me to follow her as she creeps up to the door.

It slides silently open, making barely more than a whisper. Beyond, the corridor is empty. The floor is hardwood, so Ilmu puts a finger to her lips to signify silence and points to the floor. I nod, although I'm not taking my boots off. If I need to fight, they are extremely handy to have, and they're basically the only approximation of a weapon at my disposal.

We slip down the corridor, passing more closed rice paper doors. Light from beyond shines through the paper, drawing golden squares on the floorboards.

I can't hear any voices or any noise, so I'm not sure whether there are people beyond the doors. Still, we don't make a sound, just to be safe.

We turn a corner and Ilmu stops. "Crap," she whispers.

"What?"

She points at the floor of the corridor stretching ahead

in front of us. "Chizu changed it. She's turned it into a nightingale floor."

I'm guessing there was magic involved—I can't imagine Chizu got down on her hands and knees after our interview to indulge in a little carpentry.

"What's a nightingale floor?"

"Floorboards that are assembled in a way that is designed to chirp like a nightingale at the slightest pressure. There's no way for us to get across it without making noise."

"I can help with that."

I'm reaching for the floorboards with my magic, intending to connect with them and suggest to them that they don't creak, but Ilmu calls out "No!"

I jump. "What?"

A nure onna screeches in the distance.

"Too late," Ilmu replies. "The nure onna will have tasted your magic on the air. You put out your magical signature into the air every time you use it, and they will have tasted your signature from my memories as well. They now know what you are. Run."

It is entirely possible to berate yourself for being a complete idiot while legging it for your life.

The floorboards creak and chirp beneath our pounding feet, and we are making such a racket that everyone must now know our whereabouts. Which they probably already know from the handy beacon I activated for them in using my magic.

I hear a massive amount of chirping behind me and glance back just as we turn a corner. Two nure onna are giving chase, their fat bodies slithering over the floorboards at huge speed.

We sprint through an open doorway. It's another

entrance to the huge room full of records, the one where Chizu consumed some of my memories.

"Close it," Ilmu barks.

She shimmers and drops her human glamour as I slide the door shut. Not sure what difference that makes as the door's made of paper—even I could plough through it.

In her true form, Ilmu trundles over to a section of the wall occupied by flat wooden paddles with carved handles. Her eyes flutter and roll back in her head.

Beyond the door I hear a loud shuffle underscored by chirping—the nure onna slithering closer.

"Ilmu, get a move on with whatever you're doing."

"Just one moment..."

The door explodes in a shower of wood splinters and torn up paper. I let out a squawk and jump back, hurrying to Ilmu's side, not that I expect she can do much against the large nure onna who just entered.

Man, I really wish I had my razors with me. Maybe I should make it a policy to always keep them with me, no matter what's going on. The nure onna would be unable to do anything with her hair if I had a couple cutthroat razors in my pockets.

She slithers towards us rapidly, her huge snake body undulating, the scales shimmering in the soft green light of the floating orbs.

"Ilmu," I call, starting to panic.

She's still standing by the wooden paddles, eyes fluttering. "Nearly...there."

The nure onna opens her mouth. I dig my fingers in my ears, but I still hear her screeching. My entire body goes numb and stiff. I'm frozen in place with my fingers in my ears—I couldn't have picked a more useless pose.

I desperately try to get my body moving, but it's like my muscles have turned to lead.

The nure onna slithers closer. She's almost upon us. Her forked tongue darts out, tasting the air. Her yellow, slitted eyes flash greedily.

Behind her, I see Chizu enter the room. She's walking towards us at a leisurely pace, obviously confident that we're stuck. Which I'm pretty sure we are. Whatever Ilmu's brilliant plan for escape was, it clearly sucked.

Except my tongue is also frozen in place, so I can't tell her that. And now I'm about to be taken apart like a piece of Ikea furniture. My thoughts flash to Hunter. Who will take care of him when I'm gone?

"There!" Ilmu exclaims. I can't see what she's doing—even my eyes are frozen in place. And they're starting to water since I can't blink.

"Get them," Chizu yells.

I feel a large paw at my arm.

And then I stagger forward, dizzy.

"I can move again," I say, shocked.

"Good, so move," Ilmu replies. "Quick."

We're standing on the edge of a rice paddy. The rice plants are still young and yellow-green, the muddy water around them so perfectly still it acts as a mirror for the palm trees at the other end.

The sky is overcast, the air still and humid.

Ilmu trots off along the packed earth edge of the rice paddy and I follow. "Where are we?" I ask.

"We're travelling in my memories, but we need to move again quickly."

"Can the nure onna travel through your memories?"

"No, but Chizu can. It will take her a while to identify the right memory, but she'll find it, eventually. All baku memories are stored in the communal record library, and since I'm here, she can access them, as she's been doing to try to find you."

I look around as I follow Ilmu. There are other rice paddies all around us, and we're headed for the only building up ahead. It's made of bamboo. Beyond it are karst peaks covered in greenery, stretching up to the sky. There are no people, no machines that I can see, no electrical cables hanging from posts anywhere in sight.

"Are we in China?" The Guilin province is known for its karst peaks. "Did we time travel?"

Before Ilmu can reply, she gives a deep shudder, groaning in pain.

And then I hear a distant screech. It's not coming from anywhere in particular, but it doesn't feel as far away as I'd like.

"Chizu has found the memory." Ilmu's panting, her body tense from the pain she must be feeling. "We don't have long. Run."

Ilmu breaks into a run, although with her lumbering body she's not very fast.

We reach the building. Inside there's very little furniture, just a small bed, a stove, and a battered old wok resting against the bamboo wall. But there is what looks like a bookcase, holding yet more wooden paddles with carved handles.

This time Ilmu doesn't need to do the odd thing with her eyes. She yanks a paddle out with her trunk. The tiny etchings in the wood glow blue.

She grabs my leg with her paw, and I gasp and stagger again, my legs feeling weak and jelly-like, my head spinning.

It's freezing cold. My breath is misting in front of my face. We're in some kind of yurt made of felt. There's an overpowering stink of something that's probably yak mixed with rancid milk. A bed is shoved against the yurt's wall, covered in a beautifully embroidered fabric all in varying shades of blue. The stove in the middle of the yurt is cold.

Ilmu barrels out of the yurt's flap, and I follow, despite how feeble my legs feel. My gut is churning painfully. Going through memories clearly doesn't agree with me.

Our yurt is in the middle of a great many others. Over to the right is a cluster of horses, and beyond them looks like some kind of desert. Mongolia—it has to be Mongolia.

I really hope we're not in Genghis Khan's era—he strikes me as the 'kill first, ask questions later' kind of guy. But thankfully the camp appears to be empty as Ilmu rushes past the yurts.

"Why are there no people anywhere?" I call after her.

"We're travelling through my memories of places. If you feel weak now, it would be so much worse if your mind had to deal with the complexities of people. That would over-whelm you. I think one baku tested full memory travel with a human man long ago. He turned into a vegetable."

Without warning, Ilmu ploughs into a yurt. There's a basket full of bamboo slats immediately to the left of the door. She grabs one, and we're off again.

This time I don't just stagger but fall to my knees, retch-ing. Ilmu was right when she said travelling through memo-ries takes its toll.

"We should have a bit of time, now," Ilmu says. She's panting hard.

She shimmers her human glamour on. Her face is drawn, and there are pink splotches on her cheeks. So her human form isn't purely an illusion—it has some tie to what's going on with her true form. I'd find that interesting if I wasn't so exhausted.

We're in a wooden house that's furnished modestly, but someone obviously took care to make it cosy. There's a stone fireplace with a massive wooden beam above it, acting as a mantlepiece. In front of it is a kind of large nest made of many cushions and swaths of fabric. Among it are wads of bloodied muslin.

A fire crackles in the hearth as if the cabin's occupant has only just left. In spite of the bloody rags, the scene feels oddly cozy.

"You okay?" Ilmu asks.

I nod—I'm still on my knees. My stomach seems to believe I'm on a boat in a rough sea. My legs don't feel like they could carry me right now.

Ilmu pulls something out of her pocket. "This is the jade piece you found in my office, right?"

"Where did you get it from?"

"You had it with you when the nure onna brought you. I managed to grab it before anyone noticed it."

Finally, some good news. "Keng Po said it was a key to the baku's realm—can we use it to get out?"

"We will need it for you to get out, yes. But we can't do that from here. We have to get back, but first we need to go a bit deeper."

"Deeper?"

Ilmu grunts, her face scrunching in pain. Her body shakes, and for a moment I think she's about to have a fit, but she gets control of herself.

Dark rings have appeared below her eyes, the mottled quality to her skin worsening.

"Deeper into my memories," she says, once again panting hard as if she's just run. "I can move through them faster and more effortlessly than Chizu, especially if she's bringing a nure onna with her. The deeper—the more memories we jump through—the heavier and slower it will be for her. Then when she's several layers deep, we hop back too fast for her to follow. And *then* we get out. That's why we had to wait for the tides, so there would be less nure onna. But it will still be tricky to get past them."

I'm not going to lie, my stomach clenches painfully at the mention of jumping through more memories. "What about what this will do to you? Isn't it painful to have me here?"

"No, because I am the one bringing you. Chizu following us, however...Here, have some water. It will help." She grabs a ladle that was resting in a wooden bucket, and pours some water into two ceramic cups.

It's fresh and tastes like it's just come out of a mountain spring. And Ilmu was right, it does help clear the cramping in my stomach.

"Are you ready?" Ilmu asks.

No, is the answer to that, but I nod all the same. My entire body groans as I stand up and follow as she walks over to a bookcase that's covered in various carved animals and shimmers back to her true form.

I throw a quick glance back around the room.

It would be prying of me to ask what this place is. And for some reason the nest of cushions and bloody rags by the fireplace doesn't strike me as the scene of violence or death. Yes, it really does feel intimate, cozy. I don't dare reach out with my magic, though, not after the disaster earlier.

Ilmu grabs a bamboo slat from the bookcase, and I place my hand on her back, fingers curling into the thick brown fur.

We jump to a deserted beach with black sands. I fall back on my ass, only just managing to stop myself from throwing up. My back aches, and my arms feel like I've done fifty press-ups.

Behind us is a forest, and in the distance is a volcano emitting huge clouds of ash. We're in a Panong, some time in the past, back when the volcano at the centre of the island was erupting.

Ilmu is digging into the sand with both large front paws, sending it flying behind her in black sprays. Using her trunk, she hauls a wooden box out of the sand.

Inside are yet more bamboo slats. I don't have the energy to stand up, so I crawl on all fours over to her, grabbing her back leg as she takes hold of a slat.

Next we land in a large, grassy plain, through which are scattered enormous stone urns. The plain of jars. We're in Laos. Ilmu finds bamboo slats inside one of them.

No one has been able to solve the mystery of the jars and why they have been scattered through the plain. Are they a baku artefact? I'm too exhausted to ask, though.

I have time for one final look before we're off again.

By the time we reach our next destination, my head is buzzing and my vision is blurry. I'm breathing heavily, and from the stink, I've obviously thrown up on myself.

A look down confirms that, yep, that's sick all on my t-shirt. Fantastic.

"Ilmu, I need a break," I croak.

But Ilmu doesn't seem to have heard me. She's collapsed on the ground and is having a full-blown fit.

12

"Ilmu? Ilmu!" She's flickering between human and true form.

I try to grab her limbs to minimise their flailing, unsure how to help her. I find myself alternatively holding on to fur or clothing.

"Ilmu?"

She comes to wearing her human glamour. "No..." she whispers.

"What happened?"

She gets on her knees. She looks devastated as she takes in our surroundings. "No, no, no."

I blink a few times, my vision clearing. We're on the edge of a lake. It's autumn, the trees all golden and orange. In the middle of the lake is a red, five-tiered pagoda that's reaching up towards the sky. The placid water's surface reflects it so perfectly, it's almost as if there's another pagoda inside the lake.

"No, no," Ilmu groans, closing her eyes as if in great pain.

"What's wrong? Ilmu, what happened? Are you okay?"

"My memory has been tampered with. Chizu changed it. We should have arrived by the bridge."

Ilmu looks sickened.

"What does that mean?"

"I don't know how Chizu did it. And how she could bring herself to do that. To touch another's memories like that..." A shudder passes through Ilmu's whole body. "She's more powerful and ruthless than I expected." Ilmu goes very still, and a quick spasm shivers through her. "And we don't have as much time as I thought. We need to move."

A wave of nausea washes over me at the thought of jumping to a new memory.

Ilmu stands up. "Come on. We have to get to the pagoda."

I push myself up to standing. The air is chill but I welcome the sensation against my skin. I need something that feels familiar and normal. It's weird because my senses tell me that I'm just by a normal lake. Nothing looks or feels or sounds different. And yet somehow my body knows that there is something wrong. Maybe it's picking up on the magic—although I haven't had that reaction to magic before.

Whatever it is, though, I don't know how much longer I can go on like this.

Ilmu starts to trot around the lake's edge, but I can't follow. I'm just about managing a slow walk. She makes an impatient sound, but she stops and waits for me.

"That's the problem with bringing someone with you, it always slows you down." Chizu has just materialised in front of us. And unlike me, she looks fresh as a daisy.

She's in true form and as she walks towards us, Ilmu and I seem very small and very weak.

"You tampered with my memory," Ilmu says, voice

shaking with anger. "You broke the second law, and you will have to answer for that."

"I broke no law at all. As elected leader, I have the power to interfere with memories in the case of an unstable baku."

"I'm not unstable, and we both know it," Ilmu spits.

"Aren't you? You knew what the human truly was, and you kept it to yourself. All these years. Even now, in these uncertain times, when having such an advantage on our side could change everything. Betraying our kind and our mission, that is one of the signs of instability."

"I have done nothing to betray our kind."

"You kept knowledge to yourself. Nowhere in your memories did I find anything saying that Qinglong's creation was stored in a human. You purged yourself on purpose to ensure we didn't discover the truth. I have to admit that I'm impressed with how subtly you managed it. Purging just enough to keep the human's identity secret, but not so much that we would be able to see that a purging has happened."

Ilmu doesn't reply.

"But no matter how well it was done," Chizu continues, "This is a betrayal. Not just of the baku but of all the Mayak."

"I betrayed no one. The baku don't need destruction to carry out our mission. Destruction is anathema to the accumulation of knowledge. And the Mayak don't need destruction either to thrive. You're making false accusations because you have grown ambitious and greedy for recognition. You want the baku to hold the same place as they once did—well you won't achieve that by causing destruction and most likely war. That runs the risk of destroying us all."

"You are too limited in your thinking. You always have been, Ilmu. It's your greatest fault. If humanity is subjugated, just think! Almost unlimited memories that would be ours for the consuming. Think of how much our stores would increase."

Ilmu shakes her head. While they're talking, I've been quietly backing up a little, so I'm behind Ilmu. Call me coward if you want, but I'm also not stupid. Those are two large creatures, Chizu especially, and right now I'm feeling about as weak as a minute-old lamb. Blow on me too hard and you could knock me and my jelly legs over.

Not only that, but I've experienced firsthand just how powerful a baku is. I have no idea if closeness is needed for memory consumption, or line of sight. One thing I do know is that if Chizu decides, she could wipe me clean, and that scares me more than anything.

Chizu makes an impatient trumpeting noise. "Anyway, enough of this. Stand aside, Ilmu. I'm still prepared to disregard your previous transgressions if you cooperate now. Whether you meant to or not, you still led me to Qinglong's creation, and that will count in your favour, so long as you go through a period of rehabilitation first."

The wind picks up, ruffling Ilmu's fur. Her silence is deafening, broken only by the blood pounding in my ears. If Ilmu gives me up, it's game over for me.

And I'm not ready to die. I'm not ready for 'the concept of Apiya' to stop existing.

The moment stretches on for what feels like an eternity.

And then Ilmu lowers her head in what looks like a gesture of submission. My stomach sinks, although I can't be surprised.

The consequences for Ilmu if she stays with me are looking pretty bleak.

I stumble a few paces back, cringing away from Chizu's hard stare.

Ilmu trumpets loudly and charges.

Chizu lets out a startled sound. She lowers her own head just in time.

Their foreheads ring out loudly at impact. Although they both have the head of an elephant, neither has tusks. They both rear up, large, tiger front paws wrestling with each other.

"I will take your memories for this," Chizu booms. She slams her head into Ilmu's flank, which sends her crashing back. "I will take your memories of your daughter." Chizu marches on her.

Something happens, I'm not sure what. I have no idea how baku magic works, really. But some connection is made between the two. Ilmu lets out a sound that's not a human scream. It's a raw animal sound.

Chizu continues relentlessly. Ilmu starts to shake, her human glamour flickers on and off spasmodically. The awful, raw noise continues pouring out of her mouth.

I remember the room we passed through before, the one with the nest and the bloodied rags. A birthing chamber.

Taking Ilmu's memories of her daughter is beyond cruel.

Ignoring my trembling legs, I let out a yell and charge at Chizu, shoving her with all my strength, attempting to jar or maybe break the connection. Her trunk sways, catches me on the shoulder, and I go flying.

I wasn't exaggerating before about how weak I am.

But one thing we learned in my Muay Thai gym is not to give up. To bounce back.

So bounce back I do, and this time I go on the offensive.

Chizu is too busy concentrating on Ilmu to pay much attention to me. And she probably thinks I'm no threat.

Mistake.

My legs are weak but I can still use momentum and my heavy boots to my advantage.

She swings her trunk again, but this time I'm ready. I duck and throw a high kick, catching her right in the left eye. She howls and turns her head away, taking a few steps back.

I feel the connection between her and Ilmu breaking.

I rush to Ilmu, who has settled in true form. Her breathing is ragged and uneven. I grab hold of her. "Ilmu? Ilmu! Can you make us go somewhere? Anywhere?"

She makes a low keening sound.

And then we blink out of existence.

13

W e're back, but this time we're not in a memory. We're not in any part of the real world, either.

Instead, we're in a room made of mirrors. More mirrors partition the room up, reflecting us to infinity. Except that behind us, in each reflection, is a different backdrop.

I recognise one of them as a memory we recently visited. We're still in Ilmu's memories somewhere. I think.

Ilmu sinks down to the ground. I still feel awful and weak, but I haven't thrown up on myself this time—bonus. Maybe my body is starting to adjust to this method of travelling.

I crouch next to Ilmu. "Are you okay? Ilmu, I'm so sorry. Did she take all the memories?"

She doesn't reply, curling into a ball, shivering hard. If she were Hunter, I'd stroke her to try to soothe her, but I have no idea if that's a good idea for a baku in pain.

Chizu appears, then. Clearly she can follow us wherever we go—fleeing is therefore not a solution.

I stand up and put myself between her and Ilmu. She's

not paying attention to Ilmu, though. "Thank you for reminding me that the important thing right now isn't to punish my renegade baku, but dealing with you."

I back away, looking around me for a way out, but wherever I turn there's nothing but smooth, reflective surfaces, showing me more places than I can hold in my mind.

There are no doors. No way out. Chizu's eye is a little swollen, but considering she got my boot heel in the face, she should have been a lot worse. Elephant skulls and skin are tough in the real world, and I guess magical creatures who are part elephant are also tough.

I fall back into a fighting stance, doing my best to ignore the trembling in my thighs and the nausea still roiling in my stomach. My body feels exhausted, in spite of the adrenaline pumping through my system, as if I've just run a marathon and then done a full circuit workout. "You can focus on me all you want," I tell Chizu. "You won't get to take me apart like a doll."

"You're reaching for the wrong metaphor. It will feel more like I'm cutting your power cord." Her eyes meet mine, and I know she's going to try to rip memories from me. But this time I'm ready, already reaching out with my magic.

It's just like when I dodged Sarroch's attempts at hypnotising me. At least that's what I tell myself. I can feel Chizu's magic coming at me, seeking my memories. And I push at it, suggesting it slides past me. It's not enough to stop her completely, but it is enough to startle her, which buys me the precious seconds I need.

I launch myself forward, pivot, and kick her right in the belly with the heavy tip of my boot. She roars in pain.

I may have avoided her magic, but I don't avoid her front paw as she trumpets in anger and swipes at me.

It catches me in the left ribs, and I careen back, crashing into a mirror.

Shards explode all around me, falling on me in a shower of razor blades.

My reflexes kicked in fast enough that my arms protect my face but they're now covered in cuts.

I push myself up to standing, mirror pieces sliding off me, shards crunching beneath my boots.

Chizu charges me.

I dodge, but not quite far enough—I'm running on fumes, and my legs just don't have the strength to do more than shift me a few inches to the side.

The impact of the front of Chizu's massive head catches me in the side and sends me to the floor, completely winded. I make a soft, pained whine. That definitely cracked my ribs.

The little time I take to gather myself is enough for her to reach me and curl her trunk around my neck.

"I need your human body to die so I can get at the energy Qinglong placed inside you," Chizu tells me matter-of-factly, as if she's discussing removing my shoe or something equally as mundane.

My fingers scrabble at her trunk, but it's like trying to pry off an iron band. The pressure constricts my throat, strangling me.

I choke and splutter, feeling the pressure buildup behind my eyes. I reach desperately for her eyes to try to gouge them, but her trunk is too long and my fingers fall short by just a couple of centimetres.

"Ilmu," I call, or at least I try to, but all that comes out is a faint whisper.

Ilmu is still curled and shaking, and clearly unable to help.

The pressure inside my head is growing painful, my throat and lungs are on fire, and my eyes feel like they're about to bulge out of their sockets. Black patches are swimming in my vision.

"Just let it happen," Chizu suggests. "Just let it go. You cannot stop the inevitable."

No way. No bloody way. This is not how I go. Yue didn't kill me and Chizu certainly isn't.

My hands scramble around the floor, and they finally reach what I was hoping for.

I stab her in the trunk with the mirror shard with a quick, hard jab. Chizu trumpets and rears back.

I gulp in a raw breath as I push myself up into a crouch. Chizu grabs at me with her trunk again, but I manage to avoid her. I gulp in more air, my throat painful.

The next time I don't dodge as well, and only luck saves me from getting caught. I'm too drained, too weak. All Chizu has to do is wait for me to collapse from exhaustion.

She reaches for me again. I roll to the side, bringing me next to her. I reach up and stab her in the belly in three short thrusts.

I wish I'd asked Sarroch more about how long Mayak take to heal injuries. I wish I'd asked more about the baku. Far too late for that.

Chizu screeches in pain and stumbles back.

My body is begging me to stop here. To just lie down. I try but fail to get up. I'm kneeling, holding my improvised weapon. If Chizu attacks now, I really don't think I'll have the strength to parry.

But she doesn't attack. Instead, she sinks on her haunches. She's doing the same spasmodic flickering of her human glamour as Ilmu was doing earlier. And then she slowly collapses to the floor.

Maybe this is how baku heal their injuries. At least it's bought us a bit of time.

I try to hurry to Ilmu's side, but all I manage is an awkward crawl. I finally realise that my right hand is agony. I release the mirror shard, which falls to the floor.

My palm is bleeding all over the place where the shard was biting into the skin. The adrenaline abruptly leaves me because I'm suddenly aware of the pain of all the cuts on my arms, of my cracked ribs, of the deep slices into my palm. To say nothing of the hangover from the memory hopping.

I very nearly keel over.

By some force of will I reach Ilmu and shake her, fingers burying in her fur.

"Ilmu. Ilmu? We need to go. I think I've incapacitated Chizu for a bit."

She finally lifts her head, her eyes unfocused.

"Chizu is out for now," I repeat. "We have to go."

"Chizu...what?" She looks over to the other baku. When she catches sight of Chizu her eyes go wide. "Apiya, what did you do?"

She pushes herself up quickly, her previous weakness apparently forgotten.

"I stabbed her. I don't know how long it will take her to heal, but..."

Ilmu rushes over to Chizu's side. Chizu's breathing is heavy.

"No, no." Ilmu sounds genuinely panicked. "We don't have time to get back to the temple to do the ritual."

"Do it...now," Chizu's voice is harsh.

An awful, icy chill travels down my spine as it suddenly dawns on me what I may have done. "But... But... You're supposed to be immortal, or as close as. You're supposed to be able to heal from physical wounds. Sarroch said only magic can kill a Mayak."

"The mirrors here are all made of magic," Chizu wheezes. "Fool of a human."

"Magic help, magic help me." Ilmu says. "I don't even have the strength of the temple to draw on."

"Pull yourself together," Chizu croaks. "Get it done. We cannot afford to lose my memories."

Ilmu nods. Still in her true form, she lies in front Chizu so they can make eye contact. Chizu's flank is soaked with blood now, and it's heaving up and down with each breath.

I'm so dizzy I can't breathe. Have I killed someone? Have I actually killed someone?

I can't process the thought. This can't be happening.

Ilmu begins to say words in the baku's guttural language. Chizu responds. There's a cadence to what they say which makes it clear these are ritual phrases.

"What about the fact that we're not in the real world?" I ask. "Isn't there someway we can get her back to the real world and heal her there? What about making her wounds disappear, somehow?" I'm grasping at anything I can, but my knowledge of the Mayak is so vastly insufficient.

"Quiet," Ilmu murmurs, her gaze locked on Chizu's.

A shiver passes between the two of them, and they both begin to flicker at the same rhythm. But it's not like earlier, when Ilmu was screaming and I could sense something being ripped away from her. Instead it's like an easing, something flowing from Chizu to her.

I bury my head in my hands. It never occurred to me that I could kill a Mayak, never in a million years. Not weak little me.

I've never killed before, although I've never had an issue with defending myself when needed. If you'd asked me in the past whether I was prepared to kill to save my own life, I probably would have said yes. I thought of myself as a badass in that way.

But thinking about killing in theory and finding yourself confronted with the reality of having taken a life are worlds apart.

My ears are buzzing and my eyes are filling with tears. I don't even like to kill the spiders I find in my house. I'm always careful not to step on ants as they bustle about their business. I've never killed a cockroach in my life, and I've taken in every animal I've come across that needed help or shelter.

How did I ever think I'd be capable of killing anyone? Not that I was intending to kill Chizu. But I have. I killed a baku. A creature who's hundreds, or maybe thousands of years old. A creature who's full of knowledge...

What have I done? What have I *done*?

Oh god, I'm going to be sick. My stomach heaves, but luckily, it's already empty.

My stomach stops lurching painfully, and I look back at Chizu and Ilmu. Chizu's breathing has slowed right down. She and Ilmu are still locked together, and if I reach out tentatively I can just about sense the flow of magic between them.

Ilmu is still consuming Chizu's memories.

Finally, Chizu shudders, and something stops.

"All I did, I did for the good of our kind," she whispers, her voice raw. Her eyes are huge as she looks at me. "It was all for the good of the baku and the Mayak."

I force myself to hold her gaze. To hold the gaze of the creature I killed. "I..."

I want to say that I'm sorry. That I'm not a killer, that I didn't mean it, as if I could take it back like a bad insult.

I know she was trying to kill me. I know she wanted to tear me apart like a doll. I know.

But that doesn't change the fact that I can't bear the thought of what I did.

"It is what it is..." Chizu looks at Ilmu and mutters a few more words that I can't understand. Ilmu crouches low, bringing the large, flat front of her elephantine head against Chizu's.

They remain like this for a few moments.

And then with a great, shuddering breath, Chizu dies.

14

I lmu stays as she is for what feels like a long time. I don't dare move or make a noise.

And then Chizu winks out of existence.

"Where did she go?" I ask, breaking my resolution to stay silent.

"Back to the physical world. We're in the part of my magic where I store my memories."

"What does it mean that I killed someone in here? For you, I mean. Does it…"

Ilmu looks at me, but doesn't speak. Her eyes are large and haunted. It's bound to be awful for her.

I close my own eyes, as a wave of the most awful guilt washes over me.

When I re-open my eyes, Ilmu shimmers her human glamour into place. She looks exhausted and sad. Very, very sad.

"Ilmu, I'm so sorry. I honestly thought I was just injuring Chizu temporarily to buy us some time. I've never killed anyone before. I've…"

"I saw in her memories—she would have killed you. No one can blame you for defending yourself. Including me."

Well, that's in theory. Taking a life in practice is a whole other kettle of fish.

"I recovered all her memories," Ilmu continues. "Nothing was wasted."

"Does that mean you got the memories of your daughter back?"

"Yes." Ilmu looks deeply relieved.

"Your daughter..."

"She died in a confrontation with the Mundanes. I have never managed to have another young since. In that respect, baku are a bit like the pari-pari—it is difficult for us to bear young."

Which probably makes the fact that I killed Chizu that much worse.

"It's why I agreed to help Qinglong," Ilmu adds. "Having gone through the pain of losing my daughter, I could understand her desperation to keep you in existence. Hold on a moment. I can't give you your memories back, but I can give you a derivative. Kind of like someone telling you what happened."

I feel something cold slip inside my consciousness, and my first reflex is to try to stop it.

"Just allow it," Ilmu murmurs.

The cold slowly warms up, and then suddenly I know how I met Ilmu. I can't picture it—that part is gone, but I know that my father told me about her, that I came to her office.

"We should go," Ilmu says. "There will be much work for me and my kind in the wake of Chizu passing, and it would be best if you weren't there when it begins."

I nod.

"And when you are back, you should call Sarroch."

"Sarroch?"

"Yes. It will very soon become public knowledge that you killed Chizu—there is nothing I can do to stop it. The other baku all need to be shown her final moments, so they will see. There will be outrage—you are still human, after all. And you killed a Mayak. This will get messy. You need Sarroch and Sangong, too, around you, and anyone else who will help."

Oh, bloody hell.

~

THE JOURNEY BACK IS EVEN WORSE THAN THE JOURNEY OVER, which I didn't think was possible. I pass out a couple of times, and retch more times than I can count, even though my stomach has long ago emptied itself of all its contents. My blood feels like it has been turned into needles, pricking my limbs from the inside.

We return to the baku realm exactly where we left, in the middle of that huge library.

Chizu is lying on the floor, her flank bloody, exactly as it had been back in the mirror room. Several nure onna are gathered around her, looking distressed. Their tongues dart in and out of their mouth repeatedly.

"I will be calling the other baku," Ilmu informs them. "But first Apiya will be going home."

Without Chizu around, the nure onna seem a lot more placid. No one makes any move to stop me.

Ilmu pushes the broken piece of jade into my hand and locks her eyes onto mine. She squeezes my hand tight enough for the rough side of the jade to dig into my already injured palm. I bite down the urge to make a sound.

Then she goes digging through the bamboo slats until she finds the one she's after. She pushes it in my other hand. "Think of your house."

I wake up on my living room floor, with my face next to the burning incense stick. The inside of my nose and throat is raw, as if I've been inhaling all the smoke from the incense stick—which I might well have. I'm still a little fuzzy as to whether I was physically in the baku realm.

As I take in the reassuring sight of my house, I find myself clinging to the hope that this was all a dream. Some hallucination brought on by the incense.

But the pain in my right palm as I try to sit up is very real. As are the cuts all over my forearms. The deeper cuts in my palm have started to clot, the blood that poured down my wrist and arm now dry and flaky.

I take a deep breath, and my ribs make it clear that there's a crack somewhere. I grunt in pain.

Hunter whines and comes to me, attempting to lick me. "Ow, no. Bad idea, Hunter. Bad idea."

I disentangle myself gingerly, trying to favour my ribs and then half climb, half crawl up the stairs. It takes me quite some time and a lot of yelping and wincing to clean and disinfect all my various cuts and bandage up my wounded hand.

I have no idea if infection can set in from magical mirror shards, but I'm not taking chances. From what Ilmu says, I'm going to have enough troubles that I don't need to deal with an infection on top of everything else.

Next up is some tea—ginger and lemon tea, in a possibly futile attempt to settle my stomach and my nerves.

I haven't forgotten Ilmu's advice that I should call Sarroch, but I feel nervous. I will have to tell him all that happened—

No point postponing it, though. It's like disinfecting a cut—it's best to just get it over and done with and take the sting.

I call Sarroch.

"Apiya? Everything okay?"

Suddenly, the weight of having to tell him that I killed a baku lands on me like a ton of concrete. "I need to speak to you about something." My voice wobbles.

"What happened?"

"Can you get here?"

"I'll be twenty minutes."

As I hang up, whatever energy kept me going ever since I got home drains away.

I slowly sink to the floor and bury my head in my arms. Hunter whines again, coming to lie next to me, resting his head on my foot.

How do I go back to just living a normal life? How do people do that—take a life and then just go on living their own? I took a life.

A *life*.

An old life. A life full of experiences and knowledge. I don't know why I focus on that. I'm not sure if Chizu had been a young baku it would have been less awful.

When a knock rings out at the door, I jump and groan from the pain at my ribs.

Has it already been twenty minutes? Every single one of my joints creaks as I stand up and head to the door.

"What happened?" Sarroch asks the moment I open the door, and he catches sight of me and my various cuts.

We can't get into it right away because Hunter temporarily forgets about my distress in his joy at seeing someone he recognises.

"Down, Hunter." Sarroch doesn't look amused, and

when Hunter doesn't immediately obey, he lets out a low growl.

Hunter whines and flattens himself to the ground before rolling on his back to show submission.

"You need to sit down," I tell Sarroch.

He goes very still. "Why? What happened?"

I'm too tired to stand, so I step out of my house and sit against a pillar. Dawn is brightening in the distance, brushing pink into the sky. I haven't slept all night—something to add to the tally of things that have me feeling awful.

I look at Sarroch mutely.

He finally sits down against the other pillar and faces me.

I take a breath. "I went out to check on Ilmu—"

"Oh, for crying out loud, Apiya. I told you to stay inside. What did you do? Yue found you, did she? Are you badly hurt?"

"Okay, you're gonna need to stay silent until I'm done telling you everything. If you shout and interrupt me every time I say something, we'll be here all day. On top of that, it's really not helping. Telling you what I need to tell you isn't going to be easy, so let's not make it even more difficult." I wince—talking a lot is painful.

"You *are* hurt."

"Just cracked ribs and cuts. Nothing major. Now let me talk."

Sarroch reluctantly agrees to keep quiet, but I can see from his expression that he's not happy about it.

"I went to Ilmu's office to check on her, with Chai accompanying me for safety." I tell Sarroch about finding the broken piece of jade and then coming home.

He looks relieved when I described coming back home, but his expression darkens once again when I tell him about going to Meng Po. I don't mention Tim—I'm responsible for my own actions at the end of the day, and there's nothing to be gained by also landing him in trouble.

Sarroch very nearly tries to interrupt me, but I give him a look, raising my hand to keep quiet. His lips thin, but he leans back against the pillar and stays silent.

I tell him all about how I was dragged into the baku realm, and then I stop.

"How did you—" he starts.

I shake my head. "I'm not done. There's something else you need to know. For that I need to go a bit further back."

I try to take a big breath, forgetting my ribs. I grunt, my arm covering my ribs protectively. "Oof. Just a second."

Once the pain from my ribs has faded, I tell him all about the ceremony at the Akha village, although I leave out the part about Yue appearing. That's likely to distract him, and she's not what we need to focus on right now.

Who'd have thought it—Yue is now the least of my worries.

"I see there's a lot you've been keeping from me," Sarroch says coolly.

"Mr Sangong asked me to."

"What's he got to do with it?"

I describe what I saw in Mr Sangong's memories, and Sarroch looks properly shocked.

"Mr Sangong didn't want anyone to know about my true nature for now, so I told no one. I take it you had no idea?"

Sarroch shakes his head. "None whatsoever," he murmurs. "That explains why you didn't feel quite right for a Touched. And Sangong knew all this time?" He tries but doesn't quite manage to hide a small flash of hurt from his features.

"He couldn't say anything because of a spell Qinglong

put on him to keep him from revealing to me what I am. And then he asked me to keep this information to myself until he had a better idea of what it meant for it to be out in the world."

"You don't have to justify why you didn't tell me anything." His face is carefully blank now. "Although given all I've been doing to try to keep you safe, knowing what kind of being you are would have been helpful."

"Mr Sangong—"

"I'm hardly 'the public'," Sarroch says curtly. He takes a breath and gives me an evaluating look. "Does Chai know?"

I feel my face heat up. "It's only because he was there, at the Akha village so he already knew a good part of it."

"I see." Sarroch's tone is now downright cold.

"Before you get upset with me—"

"Upset? I'm not upset."

That's a lie. "If you say so. But things are about to get a lot worse, so please bear with me."

I get back to my entry into the realm of the baku and describe Chizu's plans for me. Sarroch pales, then.

"Ilmu believes that if I am weaponised in this way to subjugate humans, magic will fall into chaos."

"Yes, I'm aware of her theory," Sarroch replies dryly. "She believes I am the inciting incident that led to the imbalance we are living in now. And she's not the only one. Although most Mayak still think me a hero for ridding the world of that species of human." He frowns at me and shakes his head. "Knowing what you truly were, how could you have gone to the baku realm and placed yourself in such danger? It would have been stupid enough as a Touched, but for what you are...You can't plead ignorance—Sangong made it clear how important it was for your true nature to remain hidden."

"I didn't—"

"I mean you took it so seriously that you kept *me* completely out of the loop, and yet you have no problem taking stupidly risky action."

For all his protests that he's not upset, Sarroch is clearly feeling something about me not telling him my true nature. If not for that, I'd be growing angry with him. I'm tired, hurting physically and emotionally, and I don't need someone calling me stupid right now.

But he's probably just lashing out because of how he feels, so I do my best to keep my tone level. After all, I'm in no position to take the moral high ground.

"Well, firstly I didn't mean to go to the realm of the baku —the nure onna dragged me in. Secondly, I didn't realise I could be dismembered like that. Mr Sangong failed to mention that. I had no idea why it might not be a good idea for my true nature to be known. You can't reasonably expect me to know things before I'm told them. Thirdly, I was trying to look out for a friend. Ilmu got herself banished because of me—I couldn't stand by, knowing she was in trouble, and do nothing."

I look at him defiantly. That part I have no regret over. I will never be the kind of person who turns away from a friend who needs help. I may have made my own situation a whole lot more complicated, but at least Ilmu is safe now.

I think. I hope.

"Anyway, it gets worse," I add.

"Worse than this?"

I nod. I plough on with my story, but the closer I get to the incident in the mirror room, the more I slow.

By the time I'm describing the fight with Chizu, every word feels heavy as lead. My throat has suddenly dried up, making it hard to form the sounds.

"She was strangling me and I... I..." I close my eyes, the memory flashing in my mind, as clear and visceral as if it was happening right now. My stomach jolts with terror and disgust.

"I grabbed a broken mirror shard and stabbed her trunk to make her release me. And then I..." There's a lump in my throat that makes it hard to swallow, and my chest is squeezed so tight that it's painful. My eyes are filling with tears and I have to blink repeatedly to swallow them back.

"I thought a wound would be... easy for her to heal. I stabbed her in the abdomen three times. I thought I was dealing with something purely physical which, as you explained, the Mayak can heal from. I thought I was just buying myself a bit of time to get away from her. Slowing her down."

Understanding dawns on Sarroch's face. "Oh, Apiya, you didn't?"

I nod mutely. "The mirrors were made of magic, apparently." I've forgotten to blink, and one of the tears spills over and rolls down my cheek. I quickly wipe it off. "She couldn't heal."

"Magic help us," Sarroch whispers.

"I didn't know," I half-wail. I hang my head. "I didn't know. I never would have done it otherwise." No blinking in the world is going to hold back the tidal wave of sadness and guilt, and just plain awfulness. I bury my face in my hands and cry.

I hear some shuffling next to me, and then a strong arm curls around my shoulders, drawing me close. I lean my head against Sarroch and just sob for a while.

15

Sarroch hands me a handkerchief.

"It's okay," I hiccup. "I have tissues inside the house."

There's enough going on right now—I don't need the added problem it would be for me to blow my nose in a clearly expensive, monogrammed, piece of pristine cotton. Hunter, who has been curled up at my feet with his head resting against my shins, comes with me, following close, looking anxious.

He'll be unsettled by all my crying and upset, poor love, so I grab him a rawhide bone from the cupboard in the kitchen. Then I get myself a few tissues, wipe my eyes, blow my nose, and splash water on my face, which makes me feel a little more human.

I still feel dreadful, but there's a definite improvement as I return outside.

"Ilmu said I needed to call you because things would get messy," I say in a small voice, sitting down next to Sarroch again.

He nods. "I sent out an urgent summons to Sangong." He sighs and shakes his head.

Guessing he's shaking his head at me, I have to respond. "I had to do something about Ilmu. Nobody seemed to care about her well-being, and the only reason she was banished was because she helped me. I couldn't have just stood by and done nothing, knowing she was in trouble. And I was right. The reason she was in trouble was because she had my old memories."

"The sentiment does you credit, even though it was completely foolish."

"What happens now?"

"Now we do our best to try to avert disaster."

MR SANGONG ARRIVES LOOKING WORRIED. I'M NOT SURE exactly how much he and Sarroch are able to communicate telepathically, but it's clear enough for him to know that something is wrong.

Sarroch brings him up to date in a few terse sentences. As he explains what happens with Chizu, Mr Sangong sighs, and his shoulders hunch.

"Oh, Apiya."

I wince. I'm starting to get a better idea of why Mr Sangong's approval means so much to me. Some part of me —maybe my subconscious, if I even have one—must remember and recognise him from that time when he kept me alive and hid me away.

Mr Sangong falls silent for a moment, obviously deep in thought. Sarroch watches him impatiently but also keeps quiet.

Then Mr Sangong squares his shoulders, having obviously come to a decision. "We need to go see Mucalinda. We have very little time before this becomes public and our hands become irrevocably tied. But there might be some way we can salvage this. If we tell Mucalinda what Apiya truly is and get her to recognise Apiya as being part of the Mayak before the news breaks, then Mayak laws about self-defence will apply. But we don't have much time, and we must do it discreetly, before anyone can intervene."

I don't ask what happens if I'm not recognised as part of the Mayak.

"WHICH WAY WILL WE TAKE HER?" SARROCH ASKS.

"The lake. It will be the most discreet way to get through to her. We can't afford anyone knowing what we're up to."

We pile into Sarroch's car, and he drives off in a screech of wheels that leaves a decent amount of rubber on the tarmac. The silence in the car is tense, broken only by the squeal of Sarroch's wheels as he drives at madman speed through the still empty streets.

The lake—the only lake in Panong—is in the middle of the island.

It's a small, volcanic lake, in the actual crater of the volcano, but for its size, it has an impressive amount of myths and legends attached to it. If Panong were any more famous on the global scene, the Loch Ness and its monster would be playing second fiddle to the host of monsters believed to inhabit the green waters of Benarung Lake.

Panong is a volcanic island but its volcano hasn't erupted in a very long time. Hikers often climb up to the crater rim, to go visit the site for offerings and prayers to the spirit of the volcano.

It is said that if anyone tries to climb the volcano without first having properly expressed respect for the volcano spirit and made offerings at its base, they will either never reach the top, or if they do, they will cause an eruption.

Which is why when we reach the official start of the trail, we're greeted by numerous shrines full of offerings.

I reach for my door handle, expecting that Sarroch will slow the car down and park it so we can begin the hike. I've climbed up Mount Benarung many times, and while the climb is certainly challenging and tiring, it's doable.

I hope Sarroch has water in the boot of his trunk, though, because in the hasty departure, I didn't think to take any. And with the heat, the hike will definitely require water.

Mr Sangong glances back at me and shakes his head. That's when I realise that Sarroch isn't slowing the car down.

Instead, he shoots through the gate, the car bouncing madly as it races up along the trail.

I gasp and wince at the damage. The car is a vintage 1960s Isuzu 117 Coupé, a sleek and beautiful Japanese car with an Italian design, and very rare. Only a limited number were made.

So to send it crashing up a mountain trail... The car squeals and creaks and protests, but Sarroch pushes it relentlessly up the steepening slope.

Luckily the trees are spaced out sparsely enough here that there is enough space for it to slip through. Branches scratch the car, vegetation tearing as it forces its way through.

That won't last, though. The trail narrows further up.

Rocks rise up to our left, the trail only just wide enough for the car to pass through but not without the bodywork sustaining some serious damage, the metal screeching as it scrapes against the rock.

I wince.

Soon the trail will grow too narrow, and we'll have to get out. Sarroch's knuckles are white as he holds on to the steering wheel, eyes staring fixedly ahead with the expression of a man possessed.

He can't seriously be expecting to drive the car all the way up to the crater rim. That's just madness, not to mention impossible.

Except that is exactly what he does. No normal car should have made it this far. When the trail grows too narrow for the car, it flips to its side, sailing through the narrow gap.

My seatbelt keeps me from crashing down, but the strap is partly across my neck, strangling me a little. I have to shift myself awkwardly and grab hold of the handle above the door to my right to get myself in a more manageable position, but there's no way to alleviate the pain in my ribs.

Neither Sarroch nor Mr Sangong seem to be affected by gravity, and Sarroch continues to stare ahead.

The car is now moving along smoothly since its wheels are no longer touching the ground.

As we climb, the vegetation becomes more sparse, going from dense forest to tall grass, bracken, and shrubs.

Sarroch flips the car back the way it was meant to be, and it lands heavily on the ground. We bounce on the suspensions, but the car continues to shoot forward, this time by the strength of the purring engine.

When Sarroch said he had stronger abilities with metal than Chai, he wasn't lying. I doubt Chai could control a moving car with the same precision, and with *three* people inside it.

We continue our mad progress up the volcano, although now it's unimpeded by vegetation. The last part brings its own challenges, the ground being overtaken by volcanic gravel that shifts beneath the car's wheel, sending them spinning.

Sarroch grunts, and the car shoots forward, increasing in speed as if the gravel wasn't there.

Okay, so it wasn't a challenge. My mistake.

He brings the car to an abrupt halt just in front of the offerings platform. And he's not even sweating or showing any sign of strain.

Powerful indeed.

I climb out of the car gingerly, dreading to see the amount of damage it sustained. For such a rare car—what a waste...

As I step out into the morning side and turn back, I'm greeted by a pristine, unblemished midnight blue car, its bodywork gleaming as if it has only just come out of the shop.

Sarroch seems entirely unbothered as he marches over to the crater's lip.

"Come on, Apiya."

I nod and hurry after him. Mr Sangong has climbed ahead.

The offerings platform is a natural, flat area on the edge of the crater lip. A plethora of spirit houses, shrines, and incense holders have been set up for people to leave their offerings.

As with every time I've come here, there are lots of incense sticks burning, fat ones that last several days. Regular incense sticks, not the kind that allow you to be dragged into another dimension.

At least I really hope so.

Food, flowers, bracelets, pretty scraps of fabric, and other trinkets are all draped over the various shrines in offering to the mountain spirit.

Beyond is the actual crater itself. The bottom of it is occupied by a lake on the side of which the volcano's vent rises up. The space taken up by the vent means that the lake has a pretty crescent shape, the water a beautiful emerald green from all the sulphur the volcano pours into it.

The rising sun has peeked over the edge, painting the crater's steep, cliff-like edges with gold. The colours are breathtaking and as with every time I've been here, I feel a real sense of awe and vastness, looking down at the lake.

Sarroch comes to stand next to Mr Sangong at the very edge of the crater's lip. Mr Sangong glances at him, nods, and then bellows something loudly in the Mayak's language that I can't understand. His voice echoes against the crater walls more loudly than simple physics and acoustics should allow.

The green waters ripple in a way that reminds me of the rippling water announcing the T-Rex in Jurassic Park. The ripples grow, and with them my nerves.

And then the platform we're standing on collapses, turning into a mass of rubble that slides at full speed down the crater walls, dragging us with it.

16

B y the time I've realised that madly falling down into the crater isn't hurting anywhere as much as it should—in fact it's not hurting at all—we've transitioned out of the Mundane world and into the Mayak.

It's night time again, but the sky is perfectly black, without any stars. The air is still, without so much as a breeze, and I can smell all sorts of dark, wet things that make me think of my pond in my courtyard, or of Kamlai, my client at the barbershop, who is an aquatic being.

We're standing at the edge of a lake—correction, we are standing *on* a lake. Standing on the water rather than sinking into it, as if this were a parable from the Bible.

The water is as black as the sky above us, and almost as smooth as glass. Despite any obvious light source, all three of us are perfectly visible and reflected in the water. There's nothing else in sight.

Neither Sarroch nor Mr Sangong look nervous as they both wait patiently, so I do my best to feel confident. And to forget that Mucalinda is such a huge, powerful being, that I found it bordering on frightening last time I saw her. If both

Mr Sangong and Sarroch expect her to help, then fingers crossed she will do so.

A hundred yards ahead, a temple slowly rises out of the water. It has numerous overlapping roofs made of gleaming blue and green tiles. They reach almost all the way to the ground on either side of the entrance.

The temple front is all of gold. We're too far away for me to make it out clearly, but I can tell that the temple's front has been worked in astounding detail. A huge set of white marble steps connect the temple to the lake's water, the steps flanked on either side by large statues of naga, serpent-like creatures.

Mucalinda is the naga-raja, the queen of the naga. Mundanes believe Mucalinda to be the king of the naga, but she in fact female, and therefore their queen. It's not uncommon for Mundanes to assume a creature is male, especially if it is ancient and powerful.

Sarroch, Mr Sangong, and I head towards the temple. As we get closer, I realise that the statues are not statues at all, but actual naga. Their scales are iridescent blue-green, a similar colour to Mucalinda's scales. They turn their heads to watch us walk up the steps, but I don't get any hostility from them. Merely vague curiosity.

Inside the temple the space is—as with almost every Mayak space I've come across—larger than the outside suggests. A huge lake surrounded by lush, tropical vegetation fills the temple, which only appears as an entrance that we're standing in.

The air is thick with humidity, as if the monsoon is about to break at any moment, and the overcast sky adds steel to the lake's blue surface. Birds and insects trill in the jungle, but the sounds are unlike anything I've come across in the Mundane world.

Unlike outside the temple, we have to wade in the water as if this were a Mundane lake. My boots sink into soft mud, and the water soon rises up to thigh level. The mud and water depth make walking difficult and awkward.

Mucalinda rises out of the water ahead of us, creating waves in the water that are high enough that one nearly knocks me over. She's an enormous seven-headed serpent, her heads towering at five metres high. The rest of her remains under the water. Her scales are iridescent, shimmering between turquoise and cobalt with a black crest all along the spine. Her belly, heads, and the tip of her tail, which pokes out of the water, are all bright red. Although there is no sunlight, her scales gleam as if she were in the midday sun.

She's both beautiful and frightening.

"So what is so important that you had to come disturb me at home?" she booms.

Her massive heads catch sight of me and slowly lower themselves towards me. She has huge fangs, each one only slightly smaller than me. I can see the pink of the inside of her mouths.

I can't help but take a step back, my heart pounding madly. Sarroch puts a hand on my shoulder, although I'm not sure if it's to stop me retreating any further or to reassure me.

"So this is the little human who has been causing such heated debates," Mucalinda says. "Who made Sarroch show emotion."

I'm not particularly keen on being referred to as 'the little human' but I'm nowhere near stupid enough to voice that thought out loud.

"We have new information for your consideration," Mr

Sangong says smoothly. "Information that, until recently, it was impossible for me to reveal."

"Impossible? Since when is anything impossible for you?" Mucalinda replies.

"One greater than me had forbidden me from speaking of it," Mr Sangong replies.

Mucalinda looks curious. "Who?"

"Qinglong."

Shock registers on her seven faces. "And why was Qinglong so interested in the little human?"

"Because Apiya is her daughter," Mr Sangong replies.

"I don't recall Qinglong ever visiting our world the way Baihu did," Mucalinda rumbles, glancing at Sarroch.

"She didn't," Sarroch agrees. "Instead, she stole little scraps of qi until she had enough to make a new entity. A daughter for herself, to alleviate her loneliness and desire for a child of her own. When the other guardians of the skies found out, they forced her to give up her daughter and demanded that the energy be restored to earth."

"So that's why we have grown so far out of balance," Mucalinda mutters, nodding to herself.

"The guardians wanted Qinglong's daughter destroyed," Mr Sangong continues, "But Qinglong felt that such destruction would not bring back balance, on the contrary."

"And of course she wanted to save her daughter," Mucalinda adds.

Mr Sangong nods in acknowledgement. "Qinglong came to me for assistance, and I agreed to help her. I infused the energy into a stillborn Mundane baby and then had a baku devour all her memories so the baby would have no idea what she had been."

Mucalinda looks at me. "Well, well."

"We need you to recognise her as part of the Mayak, oh wise one," Sarroch says.

"Once the truth of what she truly is gets out, you can see the potential for corruption," Mr Sangong adds. "She must be protected by our laws."

"Corruption?" a new voice asks. Shiva appears, smiling pleasantly. He too is far bigger than I remember, so I'm guessing Mayak Elders are able to change their size at will.

He towers so that he is of a head with Mucalinda. His skin is blue, but paler than Mucalinda's scales.

His ink-black hair gleams down his back, part of it swept back with thick gold chains. Another gold chain hangs over his bare chest. Thick gold coils encircle his biceps and wrists. He wears loose black silk trousers that gather at the ankles, just above small anklets bearing tiny bells that jingle with each footstep.

Unlike us, he can walk on the water, so his trousers remain dry.

"This is very sneaky of you, Mucalinda," he says, looking amused. "Entertaining Sarroch and his little human and attempting to get around the rest of us Elders."

"I'm attempting nothing," Mucalinda replies coldly. "And I don't appreciate you barging in uninvited, nor do I appreciate you eavesdropping."

"It is a good thing that I did, though. Because this matter isn't for you to decide alone. We should all get a chance to voice our thoughts on the matter before a final call is made on whether she can be recognised as Mayak."

I shift uncomfortably from one foot to the other as I pick up tension from both Sarroch and Mr Sangong. Neither of them liked Shiva when we last saw him at Luyang Temple, so something tells me his arrival is bad news.

17

S hiva turns to face Mr Sangong and Sarroch. Credit to them both, neither of them look frightened at finding themselves in the glare of such a large and clearly powerful being. "You mentioned the truth of who this little human truly is. Or rather she is," he says pleasantly. "What truth is that, exactly? What truth have you been keeping from the Elders?"

His tone might be pleasant, but his eyes are not. They're cold, bordering on angry.

Shiva is nicknamed Shiva The Destroyer. The Hindus believe him to be the god who destroys the old to make space for the new. The stories also speak of him having a chariot of fire. None of these things inspires confidence right now.

I mean, if the baku are normally quite peaceful and gentle creatures, and yet Chizu was prepared to have me dismembered, I can't imagine someone called The Destroyer will be in favour of keeping me in one piece.

"Shiva is right," Mucalinda booms. "You cannot ask me

to keep this hidden from the other Elders. You know this, Sangong."

"And you know what will happen, what is at stake if her true nature gets out," he replies. "Whereas if she is simply integrated as part of the Mayak, there is a real opportunity for peaceful resolution. The balance to be found once more."

"This is getting more and more interesting," Shiva says. And I really don't like the way his dark eyes look over me.

Before anyone else can speak, they all pause, eyes distant, as if listening to something. I strain to hear, but I don't pick up on anything save for a shiver of magic.

Sarroch turns to look at me, his eyes regretful. "We're too late. The baku have worked fast, and they have already made what happened to Chizu public."

Shiva smirks. "So that's why you were trying to push this through, Sangong. You wanted to protect the little murderer."

Murderer. The word slices, cold and sick, through my belly. *Murderer*. That's what I am now. What I will always be. I feel ill.

Shiva throws Mucalinda a sly look. "There would have been a time when you would have caught such a deceit, oh seven-headed one. Your weakness for Sangong blinds you."

Mucalinda raises her heads up. "I have no weakness."

"If you say so."

She turns to Mr Sangong. "But Shiva is right. You deceived me." She sounds angry. "What games are you playing, Sangong?"

"His own, as always," Shiva answers silkily, but his voice has a cold and threatening edge.

"I was simply trying to keep the peace," Mr Sangong replies. "Just think, Mucalinda. Think. Think what is at risk.

Peace is the only way we can go forward. Peace is the only way that we can restore balance to the world. And for that, we need Apiya. Recognise her. She is the daughter of one of the guardians of the skies, she deserves—"

"It does not have a gender," Shiva snaps. "It is simply energy that Qinglong gave form to. Just because you chose a female container to place that energy in, doesn't mean we need to recognise it as female."

"Qinglong referred to her as her daughter," Sangong counters. "Apiya is female and should be recognised as such."

"And while we're at it, you're asking that we recognise the energy's container as part of the Mayak," Shiva continues, as if Sangong hasn't spoken. "Why should we do that? The energy that Qinglong stole may be recognised, but we don't have to recognise a corpse. A *human* corpse."

Making it clear that the greater crime isn't that the baby Sangong chose was dead, but that she was human.

Shiva spins on his heels, but despite his massive size, the water does not even move. "This is a joke," he calls over his shoulder as he walks away. "A joke, Sangong. You're going senile in your old age that you would even think you could make this work."

Sarroch looks at the huge seven-headed snake, which is still regarding us. "Mucalinda, please. You were always in favour of peace. Nothing good will come of Apiya being destroyed."

"And I might have been able to do something had you not lied to me," Mucalinda hisses angrily. "*Lied*."

"Omitted the truth," Sarroch countered.

"Lied." Her tone brooks no answers. "Had you come to me with the truth—the *full* truth—I might have been able to do something. But you made me lose face in front of Shiva. I cannot do anything for you now."

"Mucalinda, please," Sarroch says. "We only—"

"You three will leave my domain right now. I do not want to see any of you again until the Reckoning."

The moment she has finished speaking the words, I feel a massive whomp of pressure and then we're standing in a pond, in what was once a park on the edge of the forest, not far from Old Town. It is now slowly being taken over by weeds and small trees.

I stagger, more from the shock of the change than anything else. This is nowhere near as taxing as jumping through Ilmu's memories, but it's still tiring. I blink a few times as my eyes adjust to the now bright mid-morning sunshine. They're gritting from lack of sleep.

All of our clothes are soaking wet, but by the time we climb out of the pond, Mr Sangong's cheap suit is once again dry. No such luck for my denim shorts.

"So what happens now?" I ask them both.

Sarroch sighs. "There will be a Reckoning. A trial."

I swallow and nod. "It's only fair that I face justice for what I did."

"It won't be justice, at least not the kind you're referring to," Sarroch says with a twist to his mouth.

"You mean I won't get a lawyer?"

"There is no such thing as lawyers amongst the Mayak. Anyone who is willing to speak for you will step forward and give their testimony. Anyone who is willing to speak against you will do the same. The Elders will weigh both sides and decide."

Sarroch's tone is bleak, making it clear what he thinks my chances are, but still I have to ask. "What are my chances?"

"Not good," he says abruptly. He looks away. "You aren't recognised as a Mayak, and there is no precedent for a human being forgiven for the death of the Mayak. On the contrary."

"Even if it was in self-defence? Even if—"

"None of that matters. All that matters is that you have a human part to you, and you killed a Mayak. There will be even less willingness to forgive, given the current climate."

"What kind of sentence will I face?" My voice is a whisper.

Sarroch shakes his head. "We will simply have to find some way out of this. There will be something. At the end of the day, you are the daughter of Qinglong. In a way, you are no different than I am, and I am recognised as part of the Mayak."

Mr Sangong nods. "Yes, we will have to find something." He sounds distracted. "I better go. Sarroch, you and I need to gather as many Mayak who will speak for Apiya as possible. And we don't have long." He walks away, unhurried.

I look up at Sarroch. "How long do we have?"

"Not long. But we will figure something out. We will figure something out."

The fact that he has to repeat this has me wondering whether he's trying to reassure himself. Which does nothing to reassure me.

18

W hen Sarroch said we didn't have long, he wasn't exaggerating. The reckoning is to take place that evening, with proceedings starting at dusk.

Sarroch and I have gone back to his office, and Sarroch is now working the phone with impressive focus. Sitting behind his large, glass-topped desk, in front of his floor to ceiling windows looking over Panong, he looks every inch the powerful CEO.

If you ignore the conversations he has in a non-human, guttural language over the phone with various Mayak, that is.

I turn back to the window I'm standing in front of, the one overlooking Luyang Temple. It stands out starkly, its red walls a sharp contrast to the deep green of the forest around it.

I lean my forehead against the window for a moment, closing my eyes and just feeling the smooth coolness of the glass. I need a moment. Everything is happening too fast, going from bad to worse.

Not getting a scrap of sleep last night isn't helping, nor having Shiva's words bounding around in my head. *Murderer. Little murderer.*

I give myself a beat to gather myself, no more than that. I'm not falling apart now. There will be something I can do.

I pull out my phone.

"Mmpf... Api, this better be important," Chai mutters as he picks up, his voice muffled by sleep. He's not a morning person—even though it's now late morning.

"Hey, Chai. I'm in a bit of a trouble and I need your help." It's pretty hard to keep my voice from wobbling. I wish Chai was here with me.

"Api? What happened?" He sounds alert now. "Did you go out? Damn it, I told you—"

"I'm going to bring you up to date and you're going to have to keep quiet until I'm done." I seem to be asking people to do that a lot lately. The men in my life are far too fond of sharing their opinions about my actions.

I tell him all that happened, all the way until this morning.

"Jesus." Chai sounds properly shocked.

"I know."

"Where are you now?"

"At Sarroch's office while he's trying to find as many Mayak as possible who will speak for me. I, meanwhile, am trying not to fall apart, and also trying to figure out something I can do to help things along. And I thought of some way you might be able to help me, if you're up for it?"

"Name it. What can I do?"

"This whole thing about having me recognised as part of the Mayak has been complicated because people are apparently worried about the 'precedent' it would set. Which got me to thinking, what if there's already a precedent that's either been forgotten or is being conveniently ignored? Could you contact as many Touched as you can and find out if they know a story when a human was recognised by the Mayak as—"

"It wouldn't need to be full recognition," Sarroch interrupts. "If there was a time the Mayak took care of a human, but not in thanks for something the human did, and not in the sense of a passing favour. Or if anyone did anything to mark them out as kin in any way. That might be enough. And it's an excellent idea, Apiya."

"Did you hear that?" I ask Chai.

"I did. I'm on it. I don't know of anything, but I'll start asking around. And for the reckoning, can I be there?"

I look over at Sarroch. "Can Chai attend?"

He frowns at me faintly, as if my question is a bit silly. "Of course not."

Of course. Mayak business and all that.

Chai promises to message the second he has anything remotely interesting.

I take a deep breath. Next up, contact my parents.

I don't try to call my mom's mobile phone, which will be switched off, since it's still stupid o'clock in England. I call the landline.

It rings out, and after a while goes to voicemail. It will have woken my parents up, but they might have gotten up too slowly to get to it on time. I just hang up and call again.

This time, Mum picks up.

"Apiya? Is that you?"

I might be a full-grown woman, but I feel such a rush of emotion at the sound of my mother's voice, that this time I'm unable to keep my voice from wobbling.

"I'm in trouble. I need you and Dad to help me."

The quality of the audio changes as mum puts me on loudspeaker.

"I'm on the line, pumpkin," Dad says. "What's up?"

I tell them everything, including the whole thing about killing Chizu, and about being a bundle of stolen energy infused into a dead baby.

I don't have to ask them to keep quiet when I speak.

It was like this when I finally admitted to them that I thought I might have magical abilities. I was so nervous, afraid that they would think I was a freak, irrationally worried that they would send me back to Panong.

Mum looked amused when I finished. "The way you were going on, I was expecting that you would be coming out to us. Telling us you prefer girls to boys. So I put together this whole speech in my head about being proud of you and loving you unconditionally, no matter what. Turns out it works on this occasion as well." And she gave me the speech.

Dad grabbed me into a big hug. "I was so worried you were going to tell us that you're pregnant."

And that was that. No hysterics. No questions. Nothing to make me feel bad about what I was.

And it goes much the same way this time as well, and it's one of the many reasons I absolutely adore my parents. I don't know many people who, on hearing that their daughter has killed a supernatural creature, and that she was made from a dead baby and some stolen energy, would remain completely calm and collected.

I finish by recounting our recent interview with Mucalinda, and why the fact that I acted in self-defence is unlikely to be considered.

The only thing Mum says when I finally finish is "You said we could help. What can we do?"

My mum's a bloody superstar. I'm sure she and my dad will have a lot to talk about when they're off the phone, but I'm really grateful not to have to deal with an emotional scene right now.

"I need to know any instances in myths and legends when a human was accepted as part of the Mayak. All it needs to be is the Mayak taking care of a human, or recognising the human as kin in any way."

"There are lots of stories of men being tricked into marrying various shape-shifting creatures," Dad says at once.

I relay that back to Sarroch. He shakes his head. "Tricking Mundanes is common and doesn't give that human any particular standing."

Dad changes tack at once with the myths of babies being stolen and replaced by a changeling.

I'm pretty sure I know the answer to that one, but I check with Sarroch just to be safe.

"Those babies either get found by a predator and eaten, or they are destroyed to avoid complications."

Sarroch told me about that before. How some female Mayak go a little crazed with the need to care for a young and steal a human baby.

Dad continues going through every instance he can think of off the top of his head. People getting turned to stone in Langkawi, in Malaysia—are the stones now part of the Mayak world? No.

He tries the Japanese legend of Samebito, a shark-like Mayak who cried blood and rubies over the death of a human friend. Also no. That human had first helped Samebito, and anyway, Samebito had been banished, so wasn't technically a Mayak when the story happened.

On and on the list goes. It features a surprisingly high

number of inns in the middle of nowhere where hapless travellers unwittingly find themselves face to face with a Mayak.

But none of it gives us the precedent we need.

"Okay. I will do some more in-depth digging until I find something. How much time do we have?"

"Until dusk here. Which is only a few hours away," I reply.

"I will find something," he tells me, calmly confident.

That's the thing about my dad. Incapable of finding his way around the airport, barely able to survive if my mother isn't around to make him eat, pick out his clothes, and generally keep him at least partly in the real world. And yet I wouldn't be surprised if he actually came up with something that solved this whole crisis.

At least I hope I'm right. I really, really hope I'm right.

19

S arroch continues contacting Mayak, alternating between phone and magic. The conversations don't always go that smoothly, but a few seem to be receptive to his argument that everyone needs to prioritise peace, which means not tearing me apart in order to reform my energy into some kind of weapon.

I leave the window, the sight of Luyang Temple no longer soothing. Instead, it's just a reminder of what's to come.

I grab a chair, one of those ergonomic affairs with a mesh back, wheels, and adjustable armrests. I twist it back and forth as I stare into space.

I'm exhausted, and I really need to sleep. But I'm so wired that I can barely stand to close my eyes for more than a minute.

Every so often I get a message from my father but although he keeps digging up more myths, still nothing fits.

Chai also messages—he's not having much better luck.

I stand up, suddenly hating how inactive I am. There must be something else I can do.

I turn to Sarroch as I get an idea. "What about Kamlai? Have you contacted her?" She's one of my regulars—a mom, which is an aquatic creature with scales that need regular trimming. She's also lovely and peaceful, and we get along well.

"Kamlai?" Sarroch asks. "Not yet. Give her a call." And he returns to his own conversation.

She picks up almost right away. "Apiya?"

"Kamlai. I'm sure you've heard the news..." I falter, suddenly awkward at what I have to ask. Because at the end of the day, I *did* kill someone. "We're, um... Sarroch and I are looking for Mayak who might be willing to speak at the reckoning—"

"Apiya," Kamlai interrupts. Her voice sounds rough and wet, which means she must be in true form. "Chizu was a friend. A good friend. I know there are always two sides to every story, but you cannot ask me to speak for you at the reckoning. I cannot defend the one who ended Chizu." Her tone is gentle, even though her words hit me like bricks thrown to my face.

"Of course," I manage to reply. "Thanks for explaining. I totally get it. And I'm sorry. I'm very sorry."

"I'm sure you are," she says sadly.

The line goes dead. I stare at my phone and then out of the window. The person I killed had friends. Good friends. Of course she did. It's not that I'm surprised, it's just... How can I face Kamlai again after this? To her I will always be Chizu's killer.

I let my phone slide into my lap and spin my chair back to face Luyang Temple, staring at it bleakly. I don't turn around when Sarroch comes to stand besides me and puts a hand on the back of my chair.

"The first kill is always by far the hardest. But in time it gets easier."

"First?" I ask. "This is my first and only. I'm never doing this to another living creature again. Never."

I pull my knees up to my chest for comfort. "Ilmu said that if my 'container' is destroyed, I would cease to exist." My voice is small. "Me, Apiya. Too much of me is linked to my body. She's not even sure I would still be conscious after the trauma of being ripped from my body."

"We'll do everything we can to make sure that doesn't happen," Sarroch says. "We'll find something, do something..." He makes a frustrated noise and steps away.

I hear an almighty crack and squeak in shock, spinning around. The glass top to Sarroch's desk has broken clean in half.

He looks almost as shocked as I feel. "I'm sorry. I'm very sorry. I'm losing my temper again..."

"It's fine. If I could break glass like that, I would as well."

My previous desire to do something has vanished. I just feel wretched, sad, exhausted.

"I need to go home," I say abruptly. The dog walker has the keys, so Hunter will be fine, but I need to see him. "I can't go to this reckoning without seeing Hunter first."

Sarroch looks at me. He comes to me and squeezes my shoulder. "Of course."

~

I FEEL A RUSH OF EMOTION AS WE PULL UP OUTSIDE OF MY house. A part of me is desperate to just shut the world away so I can potter with my plants and animals and pretend none of it happened. That none of it is real. I wish I could go back in time by a few days. Why did I think that house arrest was such a bad deal?

"I'll wait for you out here," Sarroch says, gesturing to his mobile. "I can't come in and I'll keep making phone calls."

I nod. "Thank you. For doing all you're doing. For helping me. I...If not for you I'd feel pretty alone right now."

Sarroch gives me the tiniest of smiles. "I guess I too don't stand by and do nothing when a friend is in need of help."

There's a beat. If he was Chai, I'd hug him right now, but he isn't Chai.

Sarroch reaches for me and pulls me into a hug, which startles me. But it's what I need right now. Even if it's only a temporary illusion, I feel safe in his arms, just for now.

Sarroch releases me, and I head to the door. Once inside, I'm greeted by a sight that's so shocking, it almost overtakes all that's recently happened.

Hunter is curled on the sofa, which is quite normal for him when I'm not home. I think he often sits there and looks at the door, waiting for me to come back, which never fails to make me feel guilty for leaving in the first place.

But keeping him company, tucked up against him in a little black fur ball, is Tim. Tim the cat. The dog-hating cat. He's cuddling Hunter.

He gets up at once, the moment Hunter catches sight of me and bounds off the sofa. "Ugh, stinking furball, invading my napping spot. Yeah, you run off, you mangy cur before I let you feel my claws for getting so close." He stretches while Hunter rushes to me, his body a frenzied wiggle of joy. I crouch down and hug him for a moment to absorb his simple joy, breathing in the comfort that he always brings.

"What would I do without you?" I whisper into the fur at the back of his neck as I hold him close—which is trickier than it sounds, given how excited he is to see me.

I look up at Tim. "I can't stay." My voice wobbles a little.

"I heard, sunshine." He sits in front of me, his tail tucking itself neatly around his paws. For once he isn't condescending or contemptuous, but instead his body language is grave. "I'm real sorry. It's a rough deal they're giving you. I'm guessing self-defence won't apply?"

I clear my throat. "It looks that way." My emotions are all over the place, and discussing all this is dangerously likely to make me cry. I'm too tired and overwrought. "I don't know how long I'll be gone."

Tim blinks slowly once. "I'll look out for the furball while you're away. Even though he stinks. And is stupid. And unbearable."

I sweep Tim up into my arms in gratitude, scratching his chin and cuddling him close. "Thank you."

Hunter enthusiastically tries to join in by leaning his paws on my belly and trying to lick Tim.

"Get off me. Get off!" Tim yelps. Although he's not clawing at me like a cat would do if he *really* wanted to be released. Still, I return him to the floor as he requested. I go to check on my menagerie.

Everything has happened so fast, I have nothing in place in case... In case nothing, I tell myself severely. Something will work out.

Everyone is quite happy, the guinea pig even more so for catching sight of me. I impulsively give him and the rabbits all the fresh salad I have left in the fridge—a real feast.

Zer is hanging out in the pond, submerged up to her nose in water.

"I'm heading out again," I tell her. "There's to be a reckoning with the Mayak. A reckoning regarding me." I'm not sure that's the proper way to phrase it. "Do you know what that is? A reckoning?" I'm not sure how much the Mayak learn from their parents, and how much is innate to them through the magic. I know a certain amount of skills and knowledge are simply passed through the magic, so ancestral memories are preserved that way.

Maybe when this is all over I should ask her parents if I should be teaching her anything more than how to hang out with a frog and how to play with Fergie the tortoise.

She doesn't react to me. Her skin is the mottled colour of an algae-covered rock, and she seems to be doing her best impression of a rock's stillness.

"I'll be back as soon as I can," I tell her. "You'll look after Fergie for me, won't you?"

Her eyes flick over to Fergie who is, for once, dozing and not climbing something. So she does understand when I talk to her. Maybe that's a recent development.

A small victory. Something to take with me, along with Hunter's adoration.

I step back into my house. "Okay," I tell Tim and Hunter. "I need to go."

"You'll be back soon," Tim says. He comes and rubs himself against my ankles. "I'm sure the furball will cover you in slobber to celebrate your return. And I'm sure I'll be pleased to see you too."

I fervently hope he's right.

20

And then it is time. I check my phone obsessively on the drive down, but nothing either my dad or Chai have managed to dig up will suit.

I have never been so obsessed with refreshing my messages. I thought I might catch a bit of sleep before the reckoning, but in the end I never managed to keep my eyes closed for long enough.

Every time I did, Chizu's final moments floated in front of my mind's eye.

"We're here," Sarroch announces. Mr Sangong is already waiting for us as we get out of the car.

I knew the reckoning would be taking place in Menara Clearing, in the south of Panong, but I expected we'd transition from there into a Mayak space that would be different —the way the barbershop or Meng Po's restaurant works. Instead, we transition into a space almost identical to the one we left in the Mundane world.

Great natural towers of rock rise up from the earth, half-covered in vegetation. In the Mundane world the towers are scattered about from whatever geological phenomenon created them. In the Mayak version, the towers mark a huge circle.

In the Mundane world, coffins that are centuries old hang from the tops of the towers. No one knows what ancient civilisation put them there or why. Theories abound —to keep the corpses safe from grave robbers, from animals, that kind of thing—but no theory fully explains why hanging the coffins instead of burying them would be more effective.

Grave robbers can also climb, after all, and most animals would have been deterred by a simple burial.

The other mystery is how the wood remained so well-preserved given that it's over a thousand years old. Well, now I know have the answer. Or at least part of the answer.

The coffins are also present in the Mayak version of the clearing. The wood must obviously have some magic to it, magic that modern technology didn't pick up on when they dated the wood of the coffins.

Why the coffins are present in both Mayak and Mundane realities, though, I have no idea. And now isn't the time to investigate.

Within the circle, crammed into the space, are a *lot* of Mayak. I look around me. Mr Sangong, Sarroch, and I are at the edge of the stone tower circle. A mist that wasn't present in the Mundane side of things hangs in the air, although I can't feel the chill or humidity of it.

It does make it hard to see very far beyond the stone towers, the mist fading into darkness. And in that darkness I sense more than see tens and tens of thousands of eyes watching.

The Mayak equivalent of the trial being filmed, I guess. And I'm to be the entertainment of the day. What do they think? Are they hostile or understanding?

"Are you ready?" Mr Sangong whispers at my side.

I swallow painfully and almost shake my head. I'm not ready at all. I feel utterly unprepared. My defence rests entirely on the nebulous concept of others speaking for me.

I check my phone again, which to my great surprise, still works. Not that there's anything on it of use.

"Apiya?" Mr Sangong asks.

"The people watching us from within the mist, will they have a say on the outcome of the trial?" I ask, not really because I care, but because I want to buy myself just a little more time.

"No, they have no vote. Only those present in person may vote on the outcome. Now, come."

And with that we walk forward, Sarroch and Mr Sangong framing me. The crowd parts to let us through, closing behind us so smoothly it feels like we're moving through a body of liquid. Other than Mr Sangong and Sarroch, every single Mayak present is in true form. Not a human glamour to be seen.

I'm not sure that's a favourable omen.

At the other side of the circle is a long raised platform. Eight Mayak sit on various seats—thrones, chairs, cushions. A ninth chair sits empty to the left. It's beautifully carved. I wonder who it's for.

Mucalinda sits in the middle, clearly presiding. She's nowhere near as large as she was when I saw her last. Same with Shiva, actually, who is a couple of seats to her right. He's much smaller, about the size of a tall man. No more than six foot three, I'd guess.

I'm not completely confident I could identify the other Mayak Elders, though. I focus on them, trying to guess who they are to distract myself from the way they are all staring at me.

There's a Chinese man wearing ample robes of pale blue. It's hard to look at him. As soon as my eyes settle on his shape, he seems to split into three, and yet I'm aware that there's only ever one of him. A trinity. I almost click my fingers. He must be the Three Pure Ones of the Tao. Or they are.

A kitsune, a fox-like creature, of the purest white with yellow gold bands at her paws and at the tips of her many, many tails, sits next to a woman with hair so long it reaches the floor where it gathers in two silky puddles on either side of her. Her face is beautiful enough to remind me of Yue, and she's clearly a vampire of some kind. Her nails are like claws, but the most startling thing about her is that her chest and abdomen are transparent, allowing a glimpse of the organs beneath.

She might be a langsuir, who legends describe as a flying head with exposed spinal cord and entrails trailing from it. They're also a type of vampire.

One Elder is looking at me with particular interest. If I didn't know he was an Elder, I'd have assumed he was a demon. His eyes bulge, and he has such huge upper and lower canines that they cause his lips to snarl. His skin is a deep, dark red, almost the colour of old blood. Of all the Elders he is the most richly attired, with a cloth of gold sarong tied by a jewelled belt at his hips, leaving his chest bare. An elaborate gold and onyx headdress sits on his head.

I don't know who he is, but as I hold his gaze for a heart-beat, I get a shiver of intuition. Death. He is related to death somehow. The moment I have the thought, I get a waft of something putrid and rotten. He smiles at me, although it's more like a pulling back of his lips to reveal more of his teeth.

"That's Berata Kala," Sarroch whispers. "One of the guardians of the underworld."

I shiver, not liking the way he's staring at me at all. I only manage to remove my eyes from him with difficulty, and I immediately feel relief as I look upon the next Elder.

Him I recognise at once. Kirin. A peaceful, gentle soul, according to legend. He's a chimera, like the baku, except that he looks like a large deer with a flaming lion's mane. Dragon scales run along his spine, all the way to his ox's tail, and his belly is also covered with bright red scales.

His face, though, is the most serene thing I have ever looked upon. Large, liquid brown eyes framed by long lashes watch me gravely. It is said he never takes a life, taking care never to tread on so much as an insect. I really, really hope he has clout with the others.

The final Elder, I also recognise. Nian, the new year demon. He looks like a deep cobalt lion with a golden mane that merges with a thick strip of golden fur that runs along his back to his tail. But while looking at Kirin immediately gave me a measure of peace, Nian gives a deeply uneasy feeling. After all, legend has it that he comes out at the new year to devour crops, livestock, people, but mostly children.

Mucalinda rumbles, but I don't understand what she's saying. Mr Sangong touches my arm and all of a sudden I can understand her words.

"...we are ready to commence, so let the human take her place."

A cushion appears before me. I'm guessing I'm supposed to kneel on it. As I'm about to step forward, Mr Sangong stops me with a hand.

"Apiya Chapman is Qinglong's daughter. She will be given the respect she is due."

"Qinglong's daughter isn't this meat sac," the vampire sneers. "She is the energy contained inside the meat sac."

I guess that answers the question of how much everyone knows.

"Lanying, surely you won't tell me you're naïve enough to assume no relationship has been formed between energy and container?" Mr Sangong asks. "No need to answer me," he adds smoothly. "A langsuir is hardly qualified to discuss such complicated matters."

Lanying's beautiful features twist in an ugly expression. "I am the Elder who represents the *predators*, Sangong. You'd do well to remember that. And remember *your* place."

"Enough!" Mucalinda booms.

"Apiya is not kneeling on the cushion," Mr Sangong says, his tone final.

"You gave up your right to influence proceedings today when you abdicated," Shiva replies.

I turn to Mr Sangong, shocked. "Did you really abdicate?" Having Mr Sangong up there might have made all the difference.

He shakes his head. "A long, long time ago. Long before you were...born."

Wait, does this mean he was a Mayak Elder?

"The human will kneel," Mucalinda orders. Even though we're outdoors and there are no walls, her voice echoes with power.

I find myself unable to resist the command, as if her voice is laced with magic. This time Mr Sangong doesn't stop me. I kneel on the cushion, which is thick enough that I'll be able to stay there for a decent amount of time quite comfortably.

I still can't believe Mr Sangong was an Elder but that he

abdicated. Why did he abdicate? Why did he become a barber?

And what kind of creature is he?

"The eight remaining Elders have come together today, in the sight of our great ancestors," Mucalinda announces. I glance at the coffins hanging overhead. "We are here for the reckoning on Apiya Chapman for killing the baku known as Chizu."

The silence is so perfect that when someone in the crowd cracks their knuckles, the sound is loud.

"As we are now but eight," Mucalinda continues, "We acknowledge that our judgement may no longer be perfect. However imperfect we are, we will endeavour to reach a justice that is clean and true and in keeping with the ancient laws of the Mayak."

A bells chimes, a single pure note that hovers far longer than it should. It vibrates in my ears. I can almost feel it against my skin.

"And so we begin," Mucalinda announces.

My stomach clenches with nerves.

21

"Since the offence was against the baku, they will begin the proceedings," Mucalinda says.

I look back over my shoulder, and out of the crowd two baku step forward. One of them is Ilmu—I recognise the markings on her tiger-striped legs. The other is about the same size as her, although the tiger-striped markings on the legs don't even reach the shoulders and hips. I can't tell if it's a male or female.

"I am Fimu, the temporary leader of the baku."

Her voice is definitely female. She bows her head to the Elders and then turns back to face everyone. "We are here today because our elected leader, Chizu, was killed. We were able to ascertain exactly what happened by looking through Chizu's final memories."

Mutters run through the crowd. Angry mutters. I feel so exposed, kneeling like this before them all.

Fimu begins giving a rundown of what happened. She's concise but precise, without skewing unreasonably against me, for which I'm grateful.

"Thank you for your account," Shiva says.

"I have something to add," Ilmu says, stepping forward. "I am Ilmu, the one who was present at Chizu's end. I would like to emphasise the fact that Apiya did what she did partly in self defence and partly to save me. This needs to hang in the balance. She may have killed a Mayak, but she saved another."

"Thank you," Shiva says curtly. "But we haven't yet opened the floor for people to come forward and speak on behalf of the accused."

"Did she truly save you?" Lanying purrs. "It didn't sound like Chizu was attempting to kill you. Just to steal the memories of your daughter. That is not a life for a life."

"My life would have been worthless without those memories. Would have been too painful to continue. I could very well have fallen into instability or madness."

Ilmu glances at me, and I give her a small, grateful smile.

"That is conjecture," Lanying says. I can kind of see her lungs moving through her transparent chest—it's really disturbing. "We do not know this for sure. After all, had Chizu succeeded in taking your memories, if she had done this so fully that you forgot you had ever had a daughter, you may have been able to produce a second daughter and thus be in a better state mentally than you are now. We have observed that Mayak who have lost a young have more difficulties in bearing another than Mayak who have never had any young."

"If you'd had young of your own, you wouldn't say something so cruel," Ilmu replies tightly.

Lanying shrugs. "It is not cruel but pragmatic. I would therefore have it be acknowledged that while Apiya Chapman rendered Ilmu a service, it is not commensurate to the crime she committed. The balance isn't fulfilled."

I guess that confirms that Lanying has already picked a side.

"We might as well open the floor to those who would come forward to speak for Apiya Chapman," Mucalinda says.

"I will start," Sarroch says, stepping forward. He gives an account of the way I saved him from Nerong.

Once he is finished, Ari comes forward. Like Sarroch and Mr Sangong, he is also wearing his human glamour. He too gives an account of how I helped him after Nerong kidnapped him.

A number of my regular clients also come to speak to my good character, each one of them wearing their human glamours, which is obviously a way to make a statement of support beyond what they're saying.

My heart is squeezed with gratitude for each one of them, and I nod in thanks to everyone, thankful they were willing to come here today. I hadn't expected so many to step forward, especially after what Kamlai said about being good friends with Chizu.

It does a great deal to lift my spirit and give me hope. It's not that I'm hoping to escape scot free—I'm not. I'm happy to face punishment for what I did to Chizu. But I don't want to die.

I glance up at the Elders—it's impossible to tell what any of them is thinking of the testimonies.

Finally, Mr Sangong steps forward. "I would also like to remind everyone present that when we decided to reveal a small number of Mayak to the Mundanes, Apiya Chapman helped us to select the most appropriate beings to go public by having her parents present helpful information to us. This was a delicate moment to navigate, and one which was made easier thanks to her help."

"It's a little early to determine whether our unveiling to the humans will have been successful and whether we have picked the right strategy," the Three Pure Ones says.

I have to look away from him because looking straight at him makes my head hurt as he seems to flicker between one and three. His voice, however, is most definitely three voices speaking as one, each at a different pitch so they harmonise together.

"What matters isn't whether or not the strategy will turn out to be successful as there are too many factors that can influence that," Mr Sangong replies. "What matters is that when we needed the help, Apiya gave it freely, as did her family."

The kitsune leans forward. If not for her many tails, she'd look exactly like a white fox. But her tails speak of her age—the kitsune wear one tail for every hundred years they've been alive. Her eyes gleam—the kitsune are known for being mischievous. Tricksters. As well as masters of illusion magic, as I discovered with Ari.

"I'm not sure what the point is of debating the accused's character," she says slyly. "At the end of the day, she isn't Mayak, is she?"

"No, she isn't," Nian rumbles. "Humans who kill Mayak *must* be destroyed. That is the rule. That has always been the rule." Drool runs out of the corner of his mouth as he stares at me.

"The matter of her status within the Mayak has yet to be resolved," Sarroch replies. "If you will remember, we still haven't finished discussing that."

"Oh, we remember," Lanying says, smirking. "How could we forget the unflappable Sarroch displaying the heart of a child for all to see?"

Sarroch's expression darkens.

This must be what Mr Sangong had referred to when he said Sarroch was getting his emotions tangled in public.

"Apiya's status became a moot point when she killed one of our own," Shiva says coldly. "It is not something that can be overlooked, no matter her previous contributions. No matter how much Sarroch embarrasses himself on her behalf. Otherwise we set a dangerous precedent. The Great Cleanse marked a new era, one in which we no longer tolerated for any human to kill our kind. We *cannot* go back on that."

Sarroch winces. All around us, people nod gravely.

"We are not suggesting that the death be overlooked," Mr Sangong says. "Nor do we suggest a step backward. Merely that the full context be taken into account. This wasn't done in cold blood, nor was it done intentionally. Apiya believed she was only wounding Chizu, not realising that the mirror pieces she used as an improvised weapon were magic and therefore deadly."

"Any human who managed to kill any of us since the Great Cleanse has been hunted and destroyed until the knowledge of how to kill us started to be forgotten or believed to be silly superstition," Shiva counters. "Now more than ever this is an essential way for us to protect ourselves. Humans have amulets allowing them to see past our glamours and to access our secret spaces. They aren't using them as weapons against us for now, but that time will come. So if we allow *any* human to kill us for *any* reason, knowledge of how to kill us will once more spread, and we will be hunted. Mark my words. And let us not forget that there are *eight billion* Mundanes. Their numbers already give them an enormous advantage. We cannot afford to give them another."

"I agree with Shiva," Lanying says. "None of this matters.

A human killed a Mayak. That human must be destroyed. There can be no argument. Word of what she did cannot be allowed to make it back to other Mundanes."

"But she's not human," Mr Sangong replies. "Or Mundane. And that is the crux of my argument. She is Qinglong's daughter—in short she is no more human than any of us. Given that, and given the circumstances, I say that while punishment is fitting, leniency should be applied."

"Why are we even arguing about this?" Berata Kala asks. The moment he speaks, the reek of death permeates everything. "She's not even fully alive. Sangong infused Qinglong's energy into a dead human—she doesn't live in the true sense of the word."

I feel like I've been gut-punched. Is that true? Am I not even truly alive? I feel alive, and my panic at the thought of dying must mean I'm alive.

Right?

I look over at Mr Sangong, but he shakes his head slightly. It takes an enormous amount of self-control to keep quiet.

"I didn't take you to be naïve, Berata Kala," Mr Sangong says dryly. "Surely you, of all people, should know the powerful bond that can be created between spirit and container. Apiya is now very much alive, because of the bond created between the energy and the body. To destroy her would be no different than destroying any other living thing."

"And we should stay clear of destruction when at all possible," Kirin says gently.

If Berata Kala stank of death when he spoke, the moment Kirin opens his mouth everyone seems to relax, and the tension in the air seems to abate somewhat. I glance back, relieved to find a number of Mayak nodding in agreement with Kirin.

"Life is precious—all life. No matter how it started, no matter what form it takes."

"We agree with Kirin," the Three Pure Ones say. "We must focus on creation, not destruction."

"You're all overlooking an important element," Lanying says. "The human container killed Chizu, well then let us destroy the human container. We won't be destroying Qinglong's daughter, then, just the host she was living in."

"But as I just pointed out," Mr Sangong replies patiently, "That will equate to destroying Qinglong's daughter due to the relationship formed between energy and container."

"It will be no worse than when you had Ilmu devour her memories when you infused her into the baby Mundane," Lanying replies. "You destroyed part of Qinglong's daughter, then, didn't you? Why would this be any worse?"

I start to panic when Mr Sangong doesn't have an answer.

"And just think," Lanying adds. "What we could do with the energy once it has been harvested and freed from the meat sac." When she speaks the words 'meat sac' she looks at me hungrily, leaving me in under no illusion what she would do with the 'meat sac' if given the chance. "We could bring the Mundanes—not just the Mundanes, all humans, including the Touched—to heel." Her eyes go wide with bloodlust at the thought, and although she's obviously far more well-mannered than Nian, I can almost feel her salivating.

"There is the problem of balance, specifically the balance needed by the magic," Mucalinda says. "I dislike this idea of subjugating humanity, because we have no idea what impact it will have on the magic."

"Mundanes are too insignificant to be able to have any real impact," Shiva says carelessly.

"But there are so many of them that their power is in their numbers," Mr Sangong replies. "They are needed for the magic to be in balance. We have always known this. We don't understand how or why, just that they are needed. And with so many of them such a massive change could end up having an enormous impact."

"So first we are afraid to go to war against them because there's too many of them, and they might win," Lanying says contemptuously. "Now we fear using a weapon that has just fallen into our laps for fear that their numbers will throw the magic into chaos. Since when did the Mayak become such cowards?"

Nian leans forward. His massive lion's body seems to bunch up, as if the muscles are coiling in anticipation of him pouncing forward.

I find myself leaning back in response, even though he's looking at Mr Sangong and not me.

"Mundanes are needed for the magic, you say. Well, I ask you, what if they're only needed as food? As fuel? You said so yourself, we don't understand how or why the magic needs the Mundanes. However, *I* need them to devour as the New Year begins, to end the old cycle and start the new. The predators need them to feed on. Berata Kala needs them for their souls. When Mundanes began to farm cattle, Nature didn't fall into chaos. It is my belief that magic will work in the same way. I believe we can farm the Mundanes."

I'm horrified to notice that a few of the other Elders are nodding their heads in agreement.

"You have no evidence to support this," Mr Sangong tells Nian. "It is purely guesswork."

"As is your theory that the magic needs Mundanes for balance," Shiva replies. "And don't forget, Sangong, that you are no longer an Elder. It is not your place to influence proceedings. Your voice is no more significant than anyone else's on the floor."

"I'm not influencing, merely offering context and advice," Mr Sangong replies carefully.

The debate continues, arguments being thrown about for both sides. I sag on my cushion, feeling more and more sure that things will not go my way.

At one point the tide turns somewhat, and things look up. But it doesn't last long before swinging back against me.

Eventually I have no idea how things are going to go. It's like a debate without any real structure. They are bouncing from one subject to another, but I'm not sure whether that means they consider the previous subjects resolved. Probably not, since they cycle back to previous subjects numerous times.

"Do you think it's going well?" I whisper to Sarroch.

He doesn't look at me. "It's far too early to tell. This will go on for a while."

He isn't exaggerating. It continues on for *hours*. My legs are slowly going numb, my ankles feeling like they are crushed beneath my weight, so I shift to sit cross-legged. And then I shift to have both knees slightly to the side so I can sit on my sit-bones and not on my ankles, the way Thai women sit when they go to the Buddhist temple.

It goes without saying that I'm a lot less graceful with it, especially in my clumpy boots.

And then I go full circle back to sitting on my heels. The fear and nerves I felt at the start of the proceedings are gradually numbed along with my legs—I don't think it's possible for a person to maintain that intensity of emotion for hours on end.

Instead, I find myself thinking of nothing as I listen to people argue about whether I should live or die. It no longer feels like they're even talking about me— rather it feels more like an abstract, philosophical debate.

Ilmu comes forward again. She's wearing her human glamour this time, as were all those who spoke for me. "I have another comment I would like to make. We all hold the Mundanes in contempt—that goes without saying. They have fallen hopelessly out of balance and have lost touch with their natural selves. Especially in the Western world. They destroy the planet they rely on to exist, they destroy their own bodies with their drugs and their drinking and their processed food, and they destroy their minds with those devices they love so much. They move through life barely alive, barely sentient, their senses too blunted to perceive anything subtle. I know this is one of the greatest arguments for the predators to be allowed to hunt without restraint, since the lives that they are hunting have so little value."

"And the one kneeling before us today is one of those Mundanes," Lanying says.

"Yes. I'm aware of that," Ilmu replies. "But shouldn't we be trying to learn from the Mundanes' mistakes rather than blindly following them?"

"An interesting riddle," the kitsune replies. "How exactly are we following them?"

"We too are falling out of balance. We baku are a peaceful, gentle folk. We are not violent nor aggressive. Yet Chizu caused me an enormous amount of pain in order to try to get her hands on Apiya, because she believed Apiya could be turned into a weapon. So many of these things are wrong for the baku. The wilful inflicting of pain on another. She threatened to report me as unstable and she even..." Ilmu gives a shudder. "She tampered with one of my memories, something that is abhorrent amongst our kind. There seemed to be no limit to how far she would go to get her hands on Apiya. That is not the behaviour of a balanced, stable baku. Especially not given that the end goal was a weapon to be used towards destruction."

"Okay, so she was unstable," Shiva says. "So what?"

"But she isn't the only one," the Three Pure Ones say, their three voices blending together harmoniously. "Yue went after a pari-pari egg. Although our laws officially don't recognise them as Mayak until they have hatched and crystallised, never in our history has one of us gone after a pari-pari egg. Although it wasn't a violation of our laws and therefore not punishable, it was a complete violation and disrespect of the pari-pari—one of our own. As a result, the pari-pari no longer consider themselves part of the Mayak, marking a new fracture among the Mayak. What if this is only the beginning? What if we too are at the start of a fall out of balance like the one the Mundanes are in the throes of? Just think for a moment. Yue's attempt to weaponise the uncrystallised pari-pari egg caused us more harm than good, because we lost the pari-pari. We don't even fully understand what that will have done to the magic yet. Or to us. What if by doing the same thing to Apiya, we cause even worse consequences? Ilmu is right. We need to get back to who we truly are, not further away from it. And we need to make sure that we don't accidentally follow in the Mundanes' footsteps."

The kitsune cocks her head. "Not all of us are creators, like you, or preservers, like Kirin," she points out, her voice sly. "Some of us are destroyers, like Shiva, and Nian. Some of us are predators like Lanying. And some of us are agents of chaos. All of these things are needed for the world to be in balance—even a little bit of chaos. Maybe chaos and destruction are what is needed to shape the world anew."

"I have something to add," a female voice says.

A shocked silence descends on the crowd, and I turn back to see who has spoken. I recognise the small pari-pari woman as the Queen who spoke at the very first mustering I attended, back when I had helped the pari-pari egg hatch and crystallise.

She has skin of a deep chocolate brown threaded with glowing copper swirls. Her eyes are slitted like a snake's and emerald-green flecked with gold. Her clothes—if they can be called that—seem to be made of iridescent turquoise and cobalt scales that match Mucalinda's. She also has the same scales covering her hands, feet, and parts of her forearms and shins, like gloves and boots. Her wings are the same brown and copper as the rest of her, but thin and a little rumpled, like those of a butterfly recently emerged from a cocoon.

A sense of earth and damp, dark, quiet places where time flows slowly flows from her.

She steps up to face the Elders.

"All the pari-pari will speak for Apiya Chapman. To begin with, she is acting as foster parent for one of our younglings. And when we needed help, she was the only one who stepped up to ensure the protection of our young. We were part of the Mayak and yet the Mayak failed to protect us. I also agree with the Three Pure Ones. For the Mayak to be willing to sacrifice one of their own young is a sign of something seriously wrong. And we the pari-pari hope the Mayak will react to this in time and not let themselves fall further into wrongness."

Shiva frowns at her. "You have decided to divorce yourself from the Mayak, so what on earth makes you think your opinion would be considered?"

"It is of no interest to me whether or not my opinion is considered, simply to make sure that I have done the right thing by coming forward and stating the pari-pari's support of Apiya. Unlike many here, we do what is right. *Not* what is convenient."

She turns and walks away abruptly before anyone else can reply. I watch her leave, but she fades away even before she's halfway through crossing the crowd.

Something has shifted in the air, something that makes me hopeful. Maybe it was the pari-pari Queen, or maybe it was a combination of her and what the Three Pure Ones and Ilmu said.

Still the discussions continue but I get the distinct impression that Lanying, Berata Kala, and Nian are not getting the same level of support from the general crowd as before.

Eventually Mucalinda raises her heads high and booms. "We have debated enough. The time has come for the vote."

The other Elders all nod, and one by one close their eyes, some of them even lowering their heads as if in concentration.

I glance over at Sarroch. "What does that mean? What are they doing?"

He shakes his head slightly. "Each Elder will...taste or sense the opinions of the crowd here tonight, and based on that, make their call. Some will even consider the opinions of those who haven't come here."

I take a shaky breath. The moment of truth has finally come. "Do you... How do you think it will go?" I whisper.

"The divide is pretty strong, but one side did not prevail obviously over the other. Still, I am...cautiously optimistic."

I'm relieved he thinks so. I close my own eyes and send a prayer to whatever entity it is that listens to prayers—if there even is anybody listening – in the hope that things don't turn out disastrously for me.

After what feels like an eternity, the Elders seem to come back to themselves, each opening their eyes.

"We will return," Mucalinda announces. And they all fade from sight.

"Now they will share their votes among themselves," Sarroch whispers. "There have been some cases where hearing the call another Elder made changes the opinion of one or two of them."

Behind me, the crowd begins to talk amongst itself, and there is a sense of restless, impatient energy as everyone waits. I can feel numerous eyes burning into my shoulder blades and sit up straighter.

I'm not going to show them any fear.

I pull out my phone and send a message to Chai and to my parents, to let them know what's going on. I'm not sure if my lack of fear stems from a sense of optimism, or simply from just how long tonight's proceedings have been going on. Maybe I've run out of fear.

Whatever it is, I feel oddly calm and prepared to accept whatever the Elders come back with.

Finally, one by one, they reappear.

"We have come to an agreement," Mucalinda booms. "Everyone has been heard, every opinion taken into account. We acknowledge that destruction could very well take us further from balance, not towards it."

Hope soars within me.

"It is therefore our intention to lean more towards peace and cohabitation in our dealing with the Mundanes than where we were before."

Nian doesn't look happy about that.

"Qinglong's energy, her daughter, will not be weaponised," Mucalinda continues.

I could honestly jump to my feet and fist bump the air, I'm so relieved. If, of course, I wasn't in front of loads of Mayak, and if my legs weren't quite so numb and stiff.

"However," Mucalinda continues, "We cannot ignore the fact that a human killed a Mayak, no matter the circumstances."

Lanying turns to me then, and she smiles. My blood runs cold.

"We have decided that only the human part of Apiya Chapman will bear the punishment in recognition that Chizu's actions towards Qinglong's daughter were wrong. The human container will be given a human's death, the energy harvested, and infused into a new container, using much the same process used by Sangong in the past, with the help of a baku to devour any lingering memories that might cause problems. That way we will ensure that Qinglong's daughter is put through no worse trauma than what she already very successfully lived through. In time she will bond with her new container like she has with this one, with no memory of Apiya Chapman. We also in this way avoid causing Qinglong any distress or offence, keeping her daughter whole and simply transferring her to a new host who hasn't committed a crime against our kind."

I stare at Mucalinda. I've heard the words, but I can't seem to understand them.

Lanying is beaming at me.

Mucalinda continues to speak, something about me being kept here until all is ready to harvest Qinglong's energy, but my ears are buzzing, and I can barely make out what Mucalinda is saying.

This cannot be happening. Mr Sangong will have some secret plan, something to get me off the hook.

But as I look up at him, I can see that his face has gone very pale. He glances down at me and I read failure in his eyes.

And guilt. A lot of guilt.

23

I'm dimly aware that Sarroch has stepped forward and is protesting loudly, but I can't focus on what he's saying. All the air seems to have left me. There are more loud voices, and finally Mucalinda booms for silence loud enough to cut through the buzzing in my ears.

I've sagged down on my cushion, as limp as a rag doll. I feel a vibration in my pocket. My mobile phone—my parents.

Oh my god, what if the Mayak don't allow me to see my parents again?

For a brief, utterly irrational moment I think of trying to run out of here, but given that I'm surrounded by powerful supernatural creatures, there is no chance I would be able to make it more than a couple of paces before I was stopped.

Maybe there is some other way. Maybe Sarroch or Mr Sangong, or someone can help me escape.

I feel eyes on me and look up to see Shiva staring at me. He shakes his head slowly at me, as if he's guessed my line of thought. I look away.

Hands shaking, I pull out my phone. It's a message from

my dad, who is still searching for a precedent of a human being recognised by the Mayak.

I need to tell him that it's too late. That it's all over, but I can't bring myself to.

Ignoring all the ruckus around me, I blink a few times to clear the tears from my eyes and read my dad's message. He's found an old folk tale that he thought might be of interest.

I feel a surge of love for him and my mother. They haven't stopped searching. Even though they're halfway across the world, and it must be late for them now, they're still searching, still trying to help.

When things are quiet enough, I'll see if I can make a phone call from here. For now, I need to send them a message. I have no idea what the hell to say, but I need to send them something, if only to feel closer to them right now.

I'm still absentmindedly reading my dad's message— which is lengthy—when I suddenly realised with a shiver of shock that Dad might have stumbled across something.

I look up to see at Sarroch, but he's gone right up near the platform where the Elders sit, arguing with them heatedly. His voice is a roar, and he looks like he might pounce on them at any moment.

"Enough of this," Mucalinda thunders. "Sarroch! Control yourself."

The air is sucked out of the space, and perfect silence blankets us all.

"Sarroch, you are overstepping yourself and embarrassing both yourself and us with your childish behaviour. The Elders have spoken, and it is not your place to question us. You *will* accept our judgement. Now, the human will be removed, to be taken for safe-keeping until we are ready to transfer Qinglong's energy. Until then, Sarroch, we will not tolerate any attempts from you to speak to Apiya Chapman or go near her. And you will *control yourself!*"

Two creatures appear on either side of me, and I'm guessing from their body language that they're here to take me away.

"Wait!" I shout, standing up awkwardly on my numb legs. "Wait, can I speak? I have just one question. I have not spoken yet on my own behalf but I would like to ask the Elders a question before I am taken away."

"Have her taken away and brought to my realm for safe-keeping," Lanying says, looking at me eagerly.

I shudder at what I read in her eyes. "One question. I believe I am allowed to speak but I haven't done so yet."

"Yes, you are allowed to speak," Mucalinda replies. "And you are right, so far you haven't said a word for yourself, which goes in your favour. So you may speak, not that it will achieve much at this point."

The blood is rushing painfully back into my legs, making it feel like an army of ants is biting them from the inside.

"Do you recognise the tale of the Tiger King as true?" I ask.

The Elders look unsure.

"It *is* true," Mr Sangong says, stepping forward.

"You are not an Elder anymore," Shiva snaps.

"No, he is not, but we believe he is right in this," the Three Pure Ones say.

"What is this tale?" Mucalinda asks.

I lick my lips. There is no time to ask Sarroch if he's willing to play along, but I have to try. It's a small sliver of hope and a massive gamble, but it's the only hope I have.

And I am *not,* I am just not ready to stop existing, no

matter if my energy or whatever would continue to exist in some other form.

"The legend speaks of a weretiger and a woman who fell in love," I say.

"There are plenty of those stories," Shiva interrupts, sounding bored. "And I fail to see what relevance they have today." He seems to have taken a special dislike to me for some reason, but I'm done being meek and quiet and taking crap.

"I have been granted permission to speak, so let me speak." I reply curtly. "The Tiger King, he was known as. He chose a human woman for his mate, but he was sent off to war against the Garuda, and he knew he would not be back for a long time. There wasn't time for the official mating ceremony to take place, but he promised that he was hers, that she was his mate, and that as soon as he returned, the ceremony would be carried out. She, in turn, promised to wait for him. She waited for seven years, seven months, and seven days. During that time famine came, along with a witch who tried to trick her into marrying another to help ease her family's need for food. There are several versions of this part of the story, which isn't important. The key point is this. The Tiger King's kin, his *sisters,* stayed nearby. They helped her through the famine, through the witch's illusions, whatever the trials are in the version of the story."

"I'm not sure how any of this is relevant to you," Kirin says gently.

"The Tiger King's sisters took care of the human woman, even though she wasn't yet officially mated. In so doing, as far as I understand it, they implicitly recognised that she was the Tiger King's mate. Which gives her a status among the Mayak, *before* the ceremony was completed."

I take a deep breath. I hope Sarroch won't be too angry

with me for this. "This establishes a relevant precedent. Because Sarroch has already chosen me for his mate. So even though it hasn't been made official by any ceremony, the Tiger King's tale means I should be recognised as already being part of the Mayak. And if I'm granted that status, then the self-defence laws apply. I cannot be killed for defending myself against Chizu. Or my container can't be killed for defending herself against Chizu—however you want to put it."

Everyone starts talking at once. Sarroch turns back to look at me. His face is pale with shock...and something else. I look back at him.

I know he never wanted to have a mate again. I know he never wanted to be involved in that way again. And that he made it clear nothing would happen with me.

But I'm desperate. It's my last shred of hope, and even if it means I'm forcing him into a corner, right now I'll do it if it means I get to live.

Mucalinda eventually calls for quiet.

"Is this true, Sarroch?" she asks. "You have chosen her for mate?"

"I find it hard to believe," the kitsune says. "Given his very public vow never to mate again."

"Sarroch?" Mucalinda asks.

Sarroch is still staring at me. His face is blank, as if he doesn't quite recognise me. My mouth has gone dry.

Please say yes. *Please.*

I don't want to die. I'm not ready to die. Please say yes.

His features briefly settle into an angry—furious—expression. His eyes icy blue, and so cold I flinch back.

And then he's composed once more. He turns away from me.

"It's true," he says stiffly.

"You chose a *human* for your mate?" Shiva asks incredulously.

"I did. Although she's not human, as we established. But as Apiya says there wasn't time for the mating ceremony."

Shocked silence reigns for a moment. And then, all of a sudden, it's like a damn opens and voices and noise pours over us.

Mucalinda raises up her heads and everyone falls quiet again.

"Well, that explains Sarroch's recent behaviour," the kitsune says. "We all know that Sarroch isn't the most rational when it comes to his mates."

I wince at how carelessly she refers to Sarroch's troubled past.

"I expect the mating to be officially completed very soon," Mucalinda tells Sarroch.

"These things cannot be rushed," Sarroch begins, but Shiva interrupts him.

"Ah, but true love knows no patience." He looks at me, and in that moment I know that he knows. "It will need to be done by the next full moon."

"Yes, that is reasonable," Mucalinda says. "But for now the precedent holds. Apiya will not be made to face the reckoning for defending herself against Chizu. According to our laws, one of ours is justified in killing in the defence of their own life. Since the baku themselves witnessed Chizu's attempt and intent to kill Apiya, she will be pardoned so long as we have a complete mating bond by the next full moon."

I could cry with relief.

And then I feel eyes on my back. I turn around to find Yue looking at me with vicious, unadulterated hatred.

24

That seems to be the signal for everyone to leave. The Elders disappear and the crowd starts to disperse.

Ilmu comes to stand next to me. "For a while there I didn't think you'd make it. I'm glad you did. From a selfish perspective, so that all my years spent banished weren't for nothing." She glances at Sarroch and looks like she wants to say something more, but she changes her mind.

Ari joins us. "I'm glad you'll be okay, Apiya." He's making quite an obvious effort not to look at Sarroch, who is also not looking at him. His body language is tense.

Then he looks over at him and their gaze locks. "This has nothing to do with you," Sarroch growls.

Ari lowers his head a fraction, a gesture of submission. "You're right it doesn't. Except for the fact that I don't think it right that you go around messing with people's lives to suit yourself."

Sarroch mentioned that Ari and Yue have some on again, off again thing going, and that Ari resents Sarroch for having bonded to Yue so she cannot ever now bond to another.

And by all accounts Yue has been presenting herself as a victim. And while what Sarroch did wasn't right, I have a hard time thinking of Yue as an innocent victim.

I'm not sure exactly what new problems my stunt will have caused, and I'll probably need time to puzzle that over.

More of my barbershop regulars come by to say hello and reiterate their support and how happy they are that I'm going to be okay. Ari slips discretely away while they talk to me.

I'm surprised by how close to emotional my customer's support gets me. I've been working with these guys for a few years now, and it really touches me to know that I matter to them.

"It would be best if you left, now," Mr Sangong whispers, coming to stand next to me. "But well done. That story is so old and obscure that most of us have forgotten it. And the Tiger King was just a regular were—not even a tiger, in fact, but a smaller, lesser cat. I forget which one. But well done for finding it."

"My dad found it."

"Hmm. Smart man."

Mr Sangong glances over at Sarroch. I follow his gaze and wince at what I see there.

"I guess you'll be coming back with me," he tells me. I don't think the arctic is as cold as his tone. A lot of people are staring at me, at us, and seeing Sarroch so angry is hardly likely to help my case.

"Yes...of course."

I want to apologise to Sarroch for pulling this on him without warning. Surely he can see that I had no other choice. But he takes my hand in a grip strong enough to be painful and drags me unceremoniously towards the exit without looking back at me.

He doesn't look at me or talk to me as we transition back to the Mundane world, either. Nor as we drive back to the Old Town.

Probably best to be in the privacy of his house to talk, anyway. Not that I'm particularly looking forward to how that discussion is going to go.

We reach his house and he storms out of the car without waiting for me. I follow, and I'm just about to reach the house door when a hand closes on my arm, yanking me back.

"So this was your plan all along?" Yue hisses. Her face is contorted with anger, so much so that for once she doesn't look movie-perfect. She actually looks ugly.

"Earn my trust. Make me think you were prepared to help me, all so I kept you alive long enough to see this come about? We had a *deal*."

"I am not in the mood for your antics, Yue. What deal did you make?" Sarroch's voice is low and dangerous.

She looks over at him, smirking. "Your mate-to-be offered me a deal. I let her live in exchange for her manipulating you into changing your mind about me. She's obviously more devious than me because I didn't see it coming that she might have been working the situation to her advantage this whole time." She smiles, but it's a smile without joy. "Well done, Sarroch. It seems you have settled for an expert manipulator after all."

Yue turns and leaves before I can answer.

I look back at Sarroch, panicked—I haven't forgotten how much he made it clear that he hated Yue trying to influence or control his emotions.

"Inside," he growls, sliding his front doors open so

violently they smack against the end of their runners, and I half expect them to break.

I scuttle in after him. "Sarroch, it wasn't like that. I wasn't going to try to manipulate you. I'm not that kind of—"

"Oh, for crying out loud, Apiya. Seriously? You tell the Mayak world that you're my chosen mate, and that's how little you understand me?"

"I..."

"Of course I know that's not what it was like, that's just Yue being Yue. But what the *hell* were you doing making deals with her in the first place? *That's* what I want to know. And *why* did you tell me nothing about it? How much more are you hiding from me?"

"I'm not hiding anything—"

"Being Qinglong's daughter, going to see Ilmu's office and finding the broken jade, making deals with Yue." He counts them out on his fingers. "That's quite the tally. Oh, and let's not forget that story you shared about the so-called Tiger King and his mate. Did it not occur to you to tell me about that earlier?"

"I only found out about it a minute before I shared it, I swear."

"Bullshit," Sarroch roars. "You keep lying to me—"

"I don't—"

"Don't you dare try to get off on the technicality that omitting isn't lying? It's lying and you *know* it!"

We're standing in the entrance hall of his house, with dark wood panelling on the lower parts of the walls and blue and white tiles on the floor. We don't stay there long, though, as Sarroch storms off through a door to the right. We enter a large and modern open-planned room that's both kitchen and living/dining room.

The counter is polished granite, and the cabinets are

sleek and white. Modern, chrome accented appliances, including an espresso machine, gleam on the kitchen countertop.

An island splits the kitchen from the rest of the space with four high bar stools along one side of it.

Sarroch marches over to the wide double fridge freezer, throws the freezer door open and grabs a bottle of Grey Goose vodka. He then grabs a glass from one of the cabinets and plonks it onto the island. His movements are so jerky and angry I'm surprised he doesn't smash the bottle or the glass.

He looks up at me, then, and his expression grows even more angry.

"Oh, that's right. How rude of me. I have a *mate* now, it seems. I guess I'll need to get a second glass."

And he does just that.

"Look, Sarroch, can we just talk for a second?"

He pours vodka into both glasses. Large, very large measures. He slides one across the island to me and downs the other.

"I thought weretigers can't get drunk?" I ask.

"It won't get me drunk, but it's something to do. Because right now I can't exactly shift and go kill something."

His eyes are growing lighter, and I can sense his tiger as if it's closer to the surface of his skin.

I take a cautious step back.

He tops up his glass with vodka, downs that too and slams the glass down so hard, the base cracks. And it's a thick base.

"So firstly, you're going to tell me all about this deal with Yue. And then you're going to tell me what else you've been keeping from me."

"That's it, I promise," I reply tiredly. I take a sip of my

vodka. I'm not a huge fan of vodka, but now doesn't seem like the time to communicate that fact. I tell him about my run in with Yue at the Akha village.

"And you didn't tell me about this because why?"

"Mr Sangong wanted me to keep quiet about my true nature so I couldn't really tell you about Yue without telling you about that too."

"Couldn't you?" Sarroch asks. It's hard to miss the sarcasm in his voice. "And after you'd told me about Qing-long, it didn't occur to you to tell me then?"

"I thought we had bigger fish to fry given what had happened with Chizu—"

"Yes, magic forbid that I be distracted by what Yue's doing and stop tending to *your* problems."

I wince. "It wasn't like that."

"Wasn't it? Then tell me what it was like. Because it seems that I'm good enough for you to announce to the world that you're my chosen mate, but not good enough for you to actually trust me with information. Did Chai know?"

"No, it's not...Did Chai know what?"

"About Yue?"

"Of course. He was there."

Sarroch goes still. "You mean the deal was witnessed?"

"Well...I mean, not really. Yue made a kind of cocoon, as if time and sound and everything stopped, and it was just her and me talking. So he was there, but I don't know if he heard it firsthand. I told him about it on the drive back, though."

"Magic help me, Apiya. You don't make a witnessed deal with a creature like Yue. Especially a deal you can't deliver on. If she can have Chai testify, she can go after you for reneging on the deal."

"But it was only a verbal—"

"Words have power. Spoken *or* written. If she can get a witness to confirm the deal took place and that you purposefully avoided fulfilling your end of it, she has grounds to go after you and exact punishment. As sanctioned by Mayak laws. For crying out loud, Apiya, it's like you're doing it on purpose!"

I've had enough of being yelled at. I'm prepared to take a lot of flak given what I've done recently, but there are limits.

"Firstly, Chai will never testify for Yue—"

"He can be compelled to do so. There's plenty of magic that can make him speak the truth."

"Which brings me to my second point," I continue hotly. I'm getting really riled up now. "You—and not just you, but all of you. Mr Sangong, Ilmu, everyone. You all seem to expect that I should know how to behave and what to do when it comes to the intricacies of how things work with the Mayak, when until recently the entirety of my involvement was limited to barbering. You tell me *nothing*, or feed me cryptic information so that I'm left always out of my depth, always a train behind, always trying to play catch up. So yeah, I play catch up in my own way, and I get it wrong sometimes. A lot of the time, recently. What do you expect? I wasn't born infused with in-depth knowledge of the nuances of Mayak society. So stop yelling at me, okay? How the hell was I supposed to know about how deals work with the Mayak if no one tells me? I'm not a mind reader."

"That's bullshit. I told you plenty," Sarroch says defensively.

"Oh really? Did you tell me anything about what was going on with the Mayak while I was stuck at home? Explained the full extent of the potential consequences if things went wrong? No."

"You didn't need to know. And if you'd done as I said and just *stayed home* we wouldn't be in this mess."

"You mean if I'd just obeyed you?"

"Yes, exactly."

Oh, I could just slap him. "And what the hell do you think gives you the right to expect obedience from me?"

"The fact that apparently you're to be my mate."

"Piss off—you don't get to pull that card on me. You have no right to expect perfect obedience from me, especially since you don't listen to me or give my opinions any weight."

"Don't play the victim, Apiya, it doesn't suit you."

"Like you listened when I told you something was wrong with Ilmu?"

Sarroch glares at me, but doesn't reply.

"If you'd listened to me and checked in with Ilmu, we wouldn't be in this mess, either. Did you think about that? I told Mr Sangong as well. I told Chai about it, too, but—"

"Of course you did, because he gets to know everything."

"Don't play jealous, Sarroch," I tell him, echoing his tone earlier. "It doesn't suit you. And don't deflect. If you all hadn't just ignored me and fobbed me off, any one of you could have helped Ilmu out. Then things would be fine."

"We were a bit busy dealing with trying to keep you safe, if you'll remember."

"No. You were a bit busy dealing with the consequences of the mess *you* created back when you bonded to Yue. You screwed all that up enough to make her utterly and madly jealous. All of it leading to where we are now. So you don't get to pin the entirety of this disaster on me. Yes, I screwed up." I lean across the island and stab him in the chest with m forefinger. "But so did you. And now we are where we are."

Sarroch's flash icy and a low growl rumbles in his throat.

I hear metallic tinkling as the metal in the kitchen is probably moving, but I don't break eye contact.

I'm *not* looking away first. I'm breathing hard, the blood pumping in my ears as if I'm about to jump across the island for a fight.

Which of course I won't do because I'm exhausted and hungry, and just generally drained from everything.

Sarroch straightens up, still maintaining eye contact. His pupils, that had contracted to pinpoints, widen slightly.

And then he looks away abruptly and lowers his head. He sighs. "You're right. If I hadn't bonded to Yue, none of this would have happened." He shakes his head. "Infinite consequences," he mutters.

He looks back at me. "This is getting us nowhere."

"I agree. We need to talk properly. Not jump at each other's throats."

"Hmm. Although at least the air feels a bit clearer now." He rolls his shoulders and cracks his neck. "Coffee?"

"Tea if you don't mind."

"Ah, yes." He gives me a small smile, and all the stuff we just threw at each other doesn't seem to matter so much anymore.

He's right, the air does feel a lot clearer.

I push the vodka across the island. "And you can have that. I'm really not a fan of neat vodka."

"You should have said."

I give him a look. "As if you would have been prepared to listen to anything from me earlier."

"Fair point."

25

We sit in Sarroch's music and library room. Where the kitchen was all bright and modern, this room is more dimly lit, more cozy. The walls are covered with books, save for one which is covered with antique wall-hangings depicting red-crowned cranes.

"When I saw these, I thought you were the owner of the Crane," I tell him.

He shrugs. "I have a thing for cranes. These wall-hangings were a gift from Yue, from back when we were still on speaking terms. She put the cranes in her club as an attempt at a peace offering, but it was far too late by then. She'd already pulled her stunt with my memories."

Sarroch puts a record on, and we each sit in one of the deep leather armchairs. The leather is butter-soft, the chair so comfortable I feel like I could sink into it and fall asleep.

"I'm sorry for the position I placed you in," I tell him. "It was never my intention. You know that, right?"

"You mean coerce me into a mating I didn't want?" he asks drily. "I know."

I stare down into my cup of tea. "I didn't want to die," I whisper. "And it seemed like the only way…"

Sarroch doesn't reply. We sit in silence for a while, listening to the jazz trumpet solo.

"I'm afraid of what the mating bond would do to me," Sarroch says at last. "Of what it might make me become again. I cannot go back to what I did, what I was for that brief time."

I don't know what to say to that. Sarroch shakes his head and rubs his face. He looks utterly miserable. I feel terrible.

I wish there had been some other way. That I knew some other werecat well enough, but calling on a customer at random instead of Sarroch was far too much of a risk. I only could play that card once. If the person I named as having chosen me for mate turned me down, I'd have had nothing else left to play.

"That's if the mating bond even takes," Sarroch adds.

"What does that mean?"

"For a mating to take, you'd have to meet my tiger. But…I don't want this. I want you to stay alive, and I want to protect you if I can. But I don't want to take a mate. So I'm not holding out much hope that my tiger will play along."

"But if I meet your tiger and it goes well, is that all we need?"

"I suppose I should explain how a mating works."

"It would be useful for me to know." Probably best if for once I was given information ahead of time so that I don't accidentally create another disaster.

"Dating, human marriage, all of that is completely separate from a proper mating bond. That just involves my human side, not my tiger."

"And a bonding is a thing involving your magic."

"Yes. Any Mayak can bond if they so choose. Only were

creatures may take a mate. The others can't have that kind of link with another."

"Okay."

"A mating bond involves both me *and* my tiger."

"Are the two of you like two separate entities?"

"Not really. More like...Two souls that are irrevocably linked."

"Do you know what your tiger thinks?"

"He doesn't think per se. He's a creature of feelings. And I can know what he feels, but if he chooses, he can shut me out. And I him. We rarely do that, though. But it happens." Something on Sarroch's face tells me that happened when they lost Eyva.

"Okay, so I meet your tiger, then what?"

"He would have to agree to you as a mate. Then you and I would also need to consummate the relationship."

"Consumate?"

"Sex, Apiya."

"Oh."

I'm not a virginal fifteen-year-old-girl to be embarrassed by the mention of sex, and yet I can't help the heat rising to my cheeks. There's something exquisitely awkward about how flat Sarroch's tone is, too. Normally my partners are not just willing, but there's at least a certain...enthusiasm.

Whereas there's no mistaking how unhappy with the situation Sarroch is.

"And then there's an official ceremony where the other werecats acknowledge you and the mate bond, at which point the bond is sealed."

I nod. That's easier and less awkward to focus on. "And what happens if your tiger doesn't choose me?"

"Then none of the rest matters. It won't work."

And then I'm back in the same position. I take a sip of

my tea. "I know you don't want this. So, is there a way that we can pretend, or..."

"No. The others will be able to tell."

Sarroch shakes his head to himself. "I can't believe I allowed things to get to this point. I had the choice of either lying and saying I'd picked you for a mate when I hadn't and didn't want to, or letting you die. And now I'm pretty sure my tiger won't want to choose you for a mate, which means I'll be caught in my lie, and you will still have to die."

I swallow. At this point I'm so far in, there's no point holding anything back. "Part of the reason I took the gamble is because Mr Sangong told me you have, um...feelings for me. In fact, he told me it was bad news and wanted me to stay away from you."

"What?" Sarroch looks irritated. "Sangong needs to mind his own business."

"He also said you are very good at lying to yourself. Anyway, when the message came through from my dad with that Tiger King tale, I thought the gamble was worth trying. On the off chance that, um, you know..." Bloody hell, this is awkward.

"Well, I guess there's only one way to find out." He puts down his cup of coffee.

For a moment I think he's going to kiss me, but he stands up.

I feel a jolt of nerves as I realise what's about to happen.

"Will you shape shift in here?"

Sarroch frowns at me. "I'm not a savage. I'll be back in fifteen minutes or so. He's always a bit sore afterwards, which makes him grumpy, so it's best if he gets a bit of time to adjust before coming back in."

"Is there anything I should do or shouldn't do? I haven't

barbered weretigers in animal form before so I'm not familiar with them..."

"So long as you make no sudden movements you'll be fine."

∼

FIFTEEN MINUTES DOESN'T SOUND LIKE A LONG TIME, UNTIL you're sitting alone in a room, waiting for a weretiger to shift because you need to meet the tiger form to see if he will choose you as a mate, and if he doesn't, you might be killed.

I check myself using my phone camera to make sure I don't look like a total disaster. My hair's looking fine, although with the soft, warm light, it looks a bit orange. But let's be honest, a weretiger is hardly going to care about that, and anyway, he's probably already seen me plenty through Sarroch's eyes.

I finish my tea. I try to look through some of Sarroch's books, but when I re-read the same title for the third time and still haven't processed what the book is, I give up.

I don't bother looking through his records. I'm clearly not in the right frame of mind for that, either. I just put the record back on when the album runs out.

And then I return to my chair and resort to various forms of knee jerking and finger tapping as I impatiently stare at the door.

When I hear heavy breathing beyond the door, I freeze. I've seen Sarroch's tiger form once before, but in very different circumstances. And from what Sarroch said, he and his tiger aren't really the same person, so it's not like I'm just seeing him in a different form.

Nerves spike in my belly as the heavy breathing grows closer and I realise I can't hear his footsteps at all.

Predators are silent and deadly, after all, and my hind-brain seems to recognise that I'm about to come face to face with a predator. I'm guessing if he didn't want me to hear his breathing, I wouldn't.

And then he's here.

He's big, far bigger than a regular tiger. His head is not quite level with mine, but it's probably level with the top of my chest.

Just at throat height if he tilts his head up. The thought makes me panic, the place where Yue cut my neck open throbbing.

His paws are huge, and as he puts one forward, the pads spread slightly to take his weight, and I can see where his retractable claws are hidden for now. His muscles bunch at his shoulders, hinting at the sheer amount of power he possesses.

His coat is silver white with black markings, and his eyes are the palest, icy blue, the colour of a glacier. Eyes that are completely focused on me. He has two huge canines that protrude from his mouth like a sabre-tooth tiger.

I go very still. Sarroch's tiger has also paused, one paw lifted as if he's about to come closer.

He lowers his paw.

Takes several deep breaths—taking in my scent, I'm guessing.

His tail is twitching slightly, as if he's irritated...or stalking prey.

I am not prey, and no matter that Sarroch and his tiger aren't the same entity, this is still a part of Sarroch in a way, so I'm certainly not going to let him scare me.

"I'm Apiya," I tell the tiger. It sounds a bit lame, but I can't think of what else to say.

The tiger moves so fast my eyes don't even register the

movement. One moment he's standing by the door, the next he's in my face. His jaws snap so close to my neck I can see saliva glistening on his fangs.

I cry out in fear and jerk back. My legs catch on the chair's armrest and I fall clumsily into it.

By the time I look back up, the tiger's tail is disappearing out the door.

Something tells me that didn't go well.

26

I'm in need of a drink. A stiff drink.

Sarroch returns, wearing a dark grey cotton yukata, a Japanese informal kimono, printed with white cranes, and held in place with a black obi belt. He also has just enough stubble for it to qualify as a beard.

The barber in me notes this—he didn't have the stubble earlier, but when werecats change back to human, it seems to come with facial hair for some reason. At least it does for the men—I haven't dealt with female weretigers, or any other kind of female werecats, actually.

A lot of Asian men can't grow a full beard, but weres don't have that problem. I had clients who came to see me very regularly so I could hack through the large, bushy beard they were left with after their change.

I realise I'm spending an inordinate amount of time focusing on Sarroch's beard and facial hair in general, probably because that's easier to contemplate than what just happened with the tiger.

I also suddenly feel seriously homesick. I miss my

simple life at the barbershop, the soothing ritual of sharpening razors and sweeping hair from tiles.

But that all seems very, very far away.

"Any chance I could get some of that vodka after all?" I ask Sarroch.

"Since you weren't a fan of it, would you prefer a whisky?" He walks over to a cabinet and opens it to display a well-stocked bar, complete with miniature icebox for the ice.

"That would be great."

He serves us both in two cut crystal tumblers. Something expensive—I'm too distracted to care what it is.

We drink in silence for a moment, the ice tinkling against the glass.

"I won't ask you whether it went well, because that part is obvious," I say. "Why was it such a disaster, though?"

Sarroch looks up from his drink and gives me a sad smile. "For two very simple reasons. You are not Eyva. You can never be Eyva. And he doesn't want to have to go through the pain of having and losing a mate again."

In short, the very same problem Yue has spent the last couple of centuries going up against. The irony isn't lost on me.

Sarroch rubs at his new stubble. "Not that I expected things to go differently." He glances at me. "Please don't take it personally. I like you, I do. A lot more than I expected to. Maybe that's what Sangong was referring to..." Sarroch frowns, considering something. "I'm not lying to myself. I just didn't want this. I don't want a mate. But it was either that or leave you to be executed, which I couldn't do. If I could take you for a mate right now, I probably would."

"And there's no way we can pretend? Just for show, for the others?"

Sarroch shakes his head. "My tiger cannot pretend or lie.

He's a primal thing of feelings, not thoughts. You are not Eyva, so that's all there is to it. We could fool some of the other Mayak, but not my brethren. The other werecats will know."

"And there's no way to talk to your tiger... Convince him, or..." I know I'm pushing him, but I'm not prepared to let it go. Because what alternative does that leave me with?

Something that doesn't bear thinking about, that's what.

"Right now? No chance. He's upset, and not just with you, with me as well."

"Why?"

"Because I considered taking another mate. Suggested to him that we should. He's not happy. And all of this made him remember her, which is never good, either."

"How long ago did she die?" I ask softly. "Hasn't it been several centuries?"

"More than that."

"And he still gets upset about the loss?"

Sarroch nods, looking down once again at his drink. "As do I." He looks up at me again, eyes wide. "I don't know how to save you, Apiya."

"We have until the full moon. So at least it's bought us a bit of time. We'll come up with something. Maybe we can find someone to help us."

"Actually, that's an idea. I never think of her, but... There is someone we could go to for help." He stands up. "I'll go get changed and then we'll go to the Tiger's Nest Monastery in Bhutan."

"Bhutan, as in the country next to Nepal?"

"As far as I'm aware, there's only one Bhutan."

"What's at the Tiger's Nest Monastery?"

"It's the entrance to the werecats' realm. We have a few

smaller ones elsewhere, including one here in Panong, but we need to go to our proper seat for what I have in mind."

I've seen photos of the monastery, an incredible series of buildings that cling to a sheer rock cliff and can only be reached by hiking up a tiny winding trail.

"We're leaving in fifteen minutes," Sarroch says decisively.

"What? No way. I need more time."

Sarroch frowns at me. "What do you need time for? You don't need to pack anything—I can get you anything you need out there."

I stand up too. "Okay, you know how before I said that you had to stop expecting me to just obey when you throw commands around?"

"You realise I'm doing this to help you?"

"I do, and I'm grateful. However, I have to see to Hunter and settle him somewhere so he will be okay without me for a time. I need to know roughly how long we will be gone to make appropriate preparations for that. I also need to find someone to take care of my other animals in my courtyard. I need to check with the pari-pari whether Zer will be okay without me, or whether she should be taken to the forest, to them. I need to talk to Chai and to my parents, who for now still don't know the outcome of the reckoning. And if I'm going to be out of signal for a while, they need to be notified." It's my turn to raise an eyebrow. "It might come as a shock to you, Sarroch, but I have a life outside of my time with you and with the Mayak."

"A very inefficient life. You should already have measures in place to take care of all this. I can arrange—"

I shake my head. "We need to find a way to make this work, Sarroch, but it won't work if you think you can just barge in and either order me around or re-arrange my life for me. Look, I don't want to be ungrateful because I'm not. I'm so thankful you're willing for us to try to work together to get out of this mess. But there are some things that are sacred. *I* take care of my animals. If I need to be away, that's fine, I can make that happen, but I need a bit of time to make arrangements."

He frowns at me, and the expression on his face telegraphs quite clearly that he's used to having his commands obeyed.

That's going to be a change for him.

"How long?"

"A few hours."

"Fine. I'll get the plane ready."

"Oh, thank god it's a plane and not some other magical way of travel. I've had my fill of that for a long time. Wait, 'you'll get the plane ready'? You have a plane?" I shake my head, remembering that he's the CEO of a big company. "Never mind. Of course you do."

"Why the tone?"

"Just that I shouldn't be surprised."

"Time is of the essence, Apiya. We're not going to waste time with a commercial flight. And I don't handle being cramped into small spaces with other humans well. It makes me hungry."

"Well then, as you fuel up the plane, be sure to pack some snacks. And tell your tiger I'm not to be on the menu."

He rolls his eyes at me. But at least the drive to my place feels a lot less tense than when we drove back to his place earlier.

"I'll come back to yours when I'm ready," I tell him as I climb out of his car. "I'll take my bike. Can I leave it parked there?"

"Sure. Just message me before you leave your place."

I nod and shut the door, heading over to my porch.

Somehow, the act of grabbing my keys from my pocket causes reality to finally sink in. I'm going to Bhutan, one of the more remote countries still left on the map, to go to the werecat's realm in order to get help engineering some kind of mating bond between Sarroch and I to keep the Mayak from carrying out their threat to execute me.

The lack of sleep these last couple of days crashes over me. I really wish I could spend the next few hours catching up, but I need to make sure the menagerie will be taken care of.

Life sure has become interesting.

Well, at least I'm still alive, and that's something to celebrate. I might as well celebrate the wins while I can, because I'm pretty sure that things are going to be equally as interesting in Bhutan, in the weretigers' realm.

THE END FOR NOW

Now Available to pre-order:

CHAINED BY MEMORY

The 6th book in the Razor's Edge Chronicles series by
Celine Jeanjean

WANT MORE?

Want to find out how Apiya met Chai, how she met Mr Sangong and started working at the barbershop?

Join the newsletter to receive Found by Rain, a prequel novella, for free.

Go to http://celinejeanjean.com/razor-bonus

ALSO BY CELINE JEANJEAN

If you want something to read in the mean time, you can dive into a whole new world that's like a mix of Victorian London and South East Asia. Discover a new cast of quirky characters, follow along their adventures and their banter, and escape into a **complete** 9 book series!

The gang's made up of:

- A skinny pickpocket with dreadlocks, a cheeky grin, and a smart mouth

- A foppish assassin with a fear of blood

- A handsome, elite fighter, master of the sardonic raised eyebrow

- A smuggler with a drinking problem and a propensity for brawling

- And a no-nonsense, heavily tattooed female machinist, trying to keep them all in line

Can they complete their missions without getting caught, killed, and without arguing?

The latter is by far the most problematic....

Check out the series over at http://celinejeanjean.com/viper-urchin/

Made in the USA
Las Vegas, NV
29 October 2021